EXODUS

Authored by
Simone K. Baker

EXODUS

Publisher:
Living With More Enterprises
www.livingwithmore.org

Cover Design:
Living With More Enterprises
www.livingwithmore.org

ISBN: 979-8-9907130-7-9

CONNECT WITH AUTHOR SIMONE K. BAKER

Website:
simonekbaker.com

Email:
simonebaker@simonekbaker.com

Facebook:
Simone K. Baker

Instagram:
simonekbaker

TikTok:
skbaker22

Dedicated to all women who have ever felt lost, confused, unsure of your worth and unseen. You're not alone. Keep walking forward; one foot in front of the other. Don't look back at your past. Focus on the bright future God has in store for you.

ACKNOWLEDGEMENTS

I would like to acknowledge those who helped this book become reality. I began writing Exodus when I was 23 years old. For 22 years I could not finish it until one day God sent me an angel who I opened up to about my book which was originally named, "Charisma." She said to me, "You haven't finished it because Charisma's story isn't over yet."

Not long after that, God gave me a word that it was time to finish the book. He told me to write one chapter a month and I would be finished by the end of the year. Well, I finished way before that. For that, I would like to thank the Holy Spirit for waking up the writer in me. For completely guiding me through this process to meet all the right people.

One of those people, specifically, is LaTrice Williams. LaTrice is my editor and publisher and has walked me step by step through this process. The late-night emails, phone calls, text messages and prayers. For that I can't thank her enough; she truly allowed God to use her.

Next, I would like to thank my family. My husband for always believing in me, for being my shoulder to lean on when times got difficult. For being the one to always speak life into me and pray over me. Honey, I love you.

To my children, Mikhala, Hailey, Aijalon, Kingston, and Princeton. To the older three, thank you for your grace in understanding that I did the best I could at being a mommy to you all, but by no means was perfect. Thank you for accepting me for where I was back then as I grew into the woman and mother I am today. To the littles, thank you for allowing mommy time away to focus on writing and for being so patient and understanding.

Thank you to my mom, Antoinette, who did the best she could, and I love her for it. To my grandma Veronica, at 94 years old, you are still my little firecracker. Thank you for being so relentless and pushing me all my life to be the best me that you knew I could be.

Finally, my church family at The Fathers House. You all are an amazing family, and I love each and every one of you so very much.

Dear Reader,

I am so glad you found this book. Or maybe this book found you. Either way, I must say, this book is not before you by coincidence.

Maybe you or someone you know has experienced some of the things Charisma experienced. Her story will help you realize you are not alone. None of us are really alone. Why do we assume in this big, big world that we are the only ones who could ever go through some of the off-the-wall life moments that some of us go through? We are not! Ladies, you are not alone.

Yes, you had that experience. Yes, you made that terrible decision that you wish no one would ever find out about. Yes, you went to that place, saw that movie, did that thing, with that person (fill in the blanks). Or maybe that terrible thing happened to you, by that terrible person, who took you to that terrible place.

All I'm saying is STOP! STOP allowing the enemy in your head. Today, he loses access to your mind. Today, you understand that you are not alone. Everything you've ever experienced, someone else has also experienced too, and it's okay.

Don't allow your past to define you. Use your past to make something great. Help another sister by letting her know you've been there too. Let's listen to one another and share our stories and help each other. If the enemy can keep us secluded, in our own thoughts, he's already won. That's where he gets us - in those shameful and alone moments. But it's when you shine light on a thing that the enemy loses his power.

I'm praying for you, sister. I'm praying for those deep, dark places of your heart that you wish would stay locked away. Those places that you hope no one will ever get access to. I encourage you to open those places up and shine a light on them. Talk to our Father about them and let Him heal you. Let Him forgive you, and you…forgive yourself. It's time to forgive yourself. You deserve it.

Let's go on this journey together and see how someone else was able to overcome her own life obstacles and find freedom. Freedom for her younger self. Freedom from her past. Freedom for her future. Freedom for her children. Freedom for me and freedom for you.

I love you, sister.
Simone K. Baker

INTRODUCTION

Charisma Hennings is a twenty-three-year-old girl from the country. She is a young girl with dreams and aspirations of being a famous poet and writer but let it all slip away.

She was raised in a middle-class family in Naples, Florida. Her mother, Lena Hennings, is a schoolteacher, and her father, Devin Hennings, owns a furniture company.

After high school, Charisma decided to go off to college. Despite the efforts of her mom and dad and their wanting her to remain closer to home at a local university, she felt it was time to move on.

Charisma was always under the protective wings of her mother and father, living in a little town in Florida. Their family was the only black family in their suburban neighborhood. She never got to see much of her own race. Never saw, for herself, the accomplishments of people who looked like her.

Besides the accomplishments of her mother and father, Charisma knew that there were people of color all over the world making a difference. People who were inventing new things and starting new businesses. She wanted to be a part of that circle.

As a young girl, growing up in Naples, Florida, Charisma was always seen as THE black girl. She was always THE black girl in the school, THE black cheerleader on the squad, THE black girl in the group of friends she hung around.

She never knew what it was like to have someone like her around. Someone she could talk to that understood her and her same issues or problems. She was tired of being the minority all her life and ready to become part of the majority.

That is why Charisma decided to attend the University of New York City. Where there were black people of all shapes, sizes, and colors.

Going off to college in New York City, to fulfill her dream of becoming a successful African American author, seemed like a dream come true. Little did Charisma know - the life she expected would not be the life she received.

In the long run, the dream turned into a nightmare. The little sheltered girl got a bite of the big apple. Better yet, the big apple took a bite out of her.

PART ONE
THE PRESENT

"Miss! Miss!"

The Greyhound bus driver shouts to the young girl sleeping in the back of the bus. Getting no response, he walks back there to try again.

"I's tell ya, these here folk can sleep through a dawg gone tornado fo cry'n out loud," the bus driver says under his breath on his way to the back of the bus.

"Miss? I said, a' Miss! We're taking a 30-minute break. Did ya wanna get out and go to da bathroom or getcha self summin'na drink before we head back out again? We gots a long ride ahead of us."

"Where are we?" She asks the stout white man standing over her. She rubs her eyes hoping and praying that her whole life is all a bad dream.

He looks at the young girl and wonders about her. He is curious about how such a beautiful girl with such a look of intelligence on her face could seem to have such a hard life. He decides to keep his thoughts and curiosities to himself and answer her.

"We're in Hickory now - Hickory, North Carolina. Nowhere near your destination, so I advise you da go on na' head and take you a break. Go grab summin'na eat or summ'n." *"Lawd knows she need it. Poor kid is skinnier than my little finga,"* the bus driver thought to himself.

As she gets her things together to go to the bathroom, the bus driver notices the tiny bulge in the young girl's tummy. He thinks to himself, *"damn, this poor girl done went ahead and got herself pregnant. When will they ever learn?"*

He asks her, "What's your name anyway, young lady?" She stops and turns around as she answers in a soft voice, "Charisma… my names Charisma."

He looks into the poor girl's light brown eyes and takes in all her pain and anguish then looks down toward her frame.

Charisma sees the pity in the bus drivers' eyes and is ashamed. She can tell that he noticed her frail body and the small bulge of her tummy. Another result of her nightmare or what some people may call - her life......

CHAPTER ONE
IN THE BEGINNING

"Charisma...that was beautiful!" Her home room teacher praises her as she heads back to her seat after reading one of her poems that she'd written. Her first class is her favorite.

Every morning, in the beginning of her advanced literature class, they had to read something they'd written. Something like a poem or something that was on their mind the day before.

Charisma always knew that she would become famous one day for her writings. From her first day of high school until now, her last week as a senior in Meadow Brook High, she'd always been praised and complimented by her teachers.

"Hey girl, have you decided what college you're going to yet?" Charisma's best friend, Brandy, asked her on their way home from school that afternoon.

"You know what college I want to go to, Brandy. Do you even have to ask that question?" Brandy did know, but she also knew that Charisma's parents would never allow it. She was kind of hoping that Charisma would have woken up by now and started looking at some other colleges.

"Brandy, why do you keep thinking that I'm gonna back down from what I love? I love New York. I've always loved New York and you know that I'm gonna go there and become famous. You've always believed in me; you know you have so don't stop now. You watch, I'll prove it. I'll prove it to you, to my mom, and to my dad. You'll see."

Brandy just looked into Charisma's hopeful face, and she couldn't admit her true feelings. Charisma was right, she had always believed in her.

She remembered when they first met back in ninth grade. Charisma was reading a poem in front of the whole class entitled, *The City Were Dreams Come True.* All through the poem, all Brandy could think was - *Wow, for a black girl, she's really smart. That poem sounds almost professional. I wonder if she stole it out of a book or something.* Brandy didn't know any better back then.

Charisma was one out of about twenty black kids in their whole entire school, and the only one in Brandy's class. So, she didn't know how to act, speak, or think about them. When all of a sudden, here is this beautiful black girl standing before her class dressed in very nice clothes, with beautiful skin, and long hair. And she was reading this awesome poem that she *claims* to have written herself. It just didn't match what she had always heard.

After class, Brandy walks over to Charisma and mocks her. "That was a nice poem you wrote. Or did you?" For a minute, Charisma thought that she was hearing things. Until it really registered in her brain that this girl was implying that she had truly stolen this poem from a book or something.

Charisma was never a fighter or a confrontational kind of person. Fighting back tears, she just stood there until she felt a burning sensation that felt like little pins poking her in the eyes. She realized that she couldn't hold them in any longer. Rather than let this racist, white girl who just insulted her work see her cry, she ran off down the hall without another word. She left her standing there in shock.

Brandy realized then that she had made a horrible mistake. She saw where Charisma took off running, straight into the girl's bathroom, and walked slowly into that direction. She could hear her crying from outside. The closer she got to the cries, the more she felt a horrible knot in her stomach. She knew that knot was her conscience.

As Brandy opened the door to the girl's bathroom, she asked, "can I come in?" Charisma wiped her face quickly and said, "It's a free country. Or is it?" Brandy knew she deserved that, but she walked toward the girl anyway. She said, "Look, I'm sorry, maybe I was wrong out there."

"Maybe!" Charisma shouted.

"Okay, Okay. I was wrong. I shouldn't have said what I said, and I'm sorry. It was just so real. Your poem, I mean. I felt like I was right there in the city as you read it. I could practically see all the lights and smell the sweet smell of spring just as you mentioned it. I just couldn't help but to think, there's no way this girl wrote that poem."

"Why? Because I'm black?" Charisma scorned.

Brandy did think that way but there was no way she was saying that to her face. She replied, "No, I mean you're in the same grade I'm in. How in the world can you write like that? I mean, it doesn't even sound like the work of a fourteen-year-old, and I do mean that in a good way."

That's when Charisma finally looked up at Brandy. She sniffed as she wiped her nose with that hard paper towel they put in the bathrooms. "So, you thought it was that good, huh," she said.

"Yeah, it was. It was really good."

Charisma couldn't hold in the effect of the compliment anymore. She released a smile that Brandy realized was truly genuine.

"So, have you ever been to New York?" Brandy asked Charisma.

"Never, but I will go there one day. I plan to become a famous writer and poet."

That's when Brandy told Charisma, "oh, it will happen. I'm sure of it. If you keep writing like that, it will happen. And I can proudly say, I knew her when she started out." They laughed together, there in the girl's bathroom, like two old friends.

Since that day, there have been countless times when Brandy would find herself comforting her newfound friend while she cried on her shoulder.

Charisma wanted so badly to go to New York to become a famous writer and live her dream. But her parents were always so protective of her. They would never allow her to even visit the city, not even for the summer. Much less to go off to school there.

Brandy used to feel sorry for Charisma. She loved her like a sister. They were practically sisters, and she always hoped that her dream would come true. At the same time, Brandy knew how sheltered of a life Charisma lived and that New York City would eat her friend alive.

But, like a good friend, Brandy kept that thought to herself as she always did. She would hug Charisma to calm her sobs and tell her, "one day sweetie, one day you'll get your wish. Don't worry, it will happen for you."

When Charisma finally reached home that afternoon, her mother handed her three envelopes with her name on them. Looking down at them, she immediately knew what they were. She just stuffed the envelopes in her backpack and kept on with her after school routine.

"So?" Her mother questioned from the hallway.

"So... what?" Charisma replies looking at her mother as if she has no clue what she's talking about.

"Well, aren't you going to open them, Charisma? They look like acceptance letters."

"I'll open them later, Mom."

"No, Charisma, you'll open them now! I'm tired of this nonsense."

"Mom, please, I just got in. I haven't even taken off my backpack yet."

"Charisma, I want you to open those letters this minute."

"Mom!" She moaned as she placed her stuff on the kitchen table.

"Mom, what!" Her mother said sternly.

Devin, Charisma's father, was coming in from the garage. He heard the commotion going on as he came through the kitchen door.

"Give her some time, Lena. She just came home from school. Wait until dinner," Devin told his wife.

"Give her some time? She doesn't have much time left."

"There's only one week of school left and what do you plan to do then, huh?"

Charisma just rolled her eyes as she grabbed an apple and headed up the stairs. She was so sick and tired of having this conversation, day in and day out.

Her father already knew what she wanted. Devin did not agree with his little girl running off to the Big City to so called become famous. But he also realized that it was something she truly wanted. So, he left all the questions alone about college.

"Charisma, I saw that!" And don't you even think that for one moment you're running off to New York City. Thinking you gonna be discovered. You need to keep your head in your books and discover what college you're going to after the summer is over. "Your daddy and I didn't raise no fool," Lena shouted up the stairs to her daughter. "You hear me, Charisma?!"

Charisma closed her door quietly and threw herself on her big king-sized canopy bed. It was one thing, knowing that her mother and father didn't want her to run off to New York to pursue her dreams. But when they actually said it, it hurt her even more. Charisma felt like if she didn't hear them saying no, then there was a chance that they would change their minds.

A couple of days would go by and no one in the house would say anything negative about New York. She would start to feel a little optimistic about her parents saying yes. Then days like this came along, and all of a sudden Charisma's hopes and dreams would melt away. Besides this situation with college, Charisma had a great relationship with her parents. So, it hurt her when they got into little altercations like this one.

Upstairs in her room, Charisma buried her face in her pillow and cried as she so often did. She thought to herself, *why do they keep treating me like a kid? I'll be eighteen years old, legally an adult, and these two won't give me that respect. They're gonna continue to treat me like a child for the rest of my life unless I stand up for myself and do something about it. I mean I've always done my homework. I always do my chores. I come home on time (when I do go out). I've never had a boyfriend, a real*

Simone K. Baker

boyfriend at least. Will they take that into consideration and give me a chance? NO!

Charisma's eyes were swollen from all the crying and her throat was sore. She sat up on the edge of her bed and looked around her room. Everything seemed so childish to her all of a sudden.

There were big, huge teddy bears neatly sitting in a hammock hanging in the corner of her room. Then there were little ballerina musical dolls all on her dresser from when she used to take ballet classes. Even the comforter on her bed had little ballerinas all over them, and little ballerina shoes. To top it all off, her walls were pink.

Instantly, Charisma became sick. She felt as if the walls of her once beautiful bedroom were closing in on her. *"This is ridiculous."* She thought to herself. *"Look at this room. I am a kid. Who am I fooling? Thinking I can run off to New York."*

That's when Charisma noticed her old journal sitting on the top of her bookshelf. One of the first journals she had ever started. She walked over to the bookshelf to look through some of her work. As she read through, she started to wonder if she really had what it took to be a professional writer. She turned the page to a poem that meant so much to her, for many reasons. The one titled, _The City Where Dreams Come True._

Charisma sat down on the edge of her bed and began to read.

>I dream of a city where lights shine bright.
>I dream of this city both day and night.

EXODUS

My love for this place runs deep in my soul,
and its love for me will never grow old.

It calls out my name, so wild and untamed.
I open my heart, as it does the same.
I answer it's plea,
Is it destiny?

To live in this place
That knows no true race.
Stars twinkle high,
Wind passes by,
Leaves start to fall,
From trees standing tall.

The beauty of each leaf
Steals your heart like a thief.
Yellow, gold, red, and green
Will have you in love like a high school teen.

Autumn skies part ever so slowly,
You know, in this city,
You will never be lonely.

This city is summer, this city is fall.
This city is winter...spring...heck, I love them all.

Charisma closed her eyes for a moment and took in every word
of her poem. She remembered the first day she ever read that

poem in front of people, and the terrible fight that followed. Then she smiled as she remembered the wonderful friendship that came of it all, between her and Brandy.

Charisma thought about how Brandy was always there for her; always a shoulder for her to lean on. Brandy never doubted that she would one day make it. For that, Charisma loved her friend dearly.

At that moment, Charisma decided that it was time. Time to take a chance and go for it. So, she announced out loud to herself in her little pink room, "I have talent. I have skills. And most important, I have a friend who is behind me one hundred and ten percent."

"I AM going to New York!!"

CHAPTER TWO
THE ANNOUNCEMENT

"Devin, Charisma! Dinner's ready, guys. Hurry up before it gets cold," Lena yelled from downstairs in the kitchen.

Charisma slowly walks down the stairs leading to the kitchen where her mother and father waited patiently for her so they could eat. Eating was the furthest thing from her mind. She had one thing and one thing only to accomplish during this meal. That was, once and for all, to tell her parents that she was going to New York.

As she reached the dinner table her heart raced. Never before had Charisma defied her parents, and what she was about to do was beyond defiance. But Charisma knew she couldn't show fear or regret in her words. She had to be strong; had to stand strong, speak strong, and look strong. Most importantly, she had to be strong or there was no way this was going to work.

Charisma took her usual seat at the dinner table with her dad at the head and her and her mother across from each other. Her father blessed the food as he always did while she said her own prayer to God.

Dear God, please let this work. I don't ask for much but I'm asking for this. Please help me. Open my mom and dad's minds and hearts to what I'm trying to say. Thank You and I love You. In Jesus name I pray. Amen.

When they opened their eyes, they saw a pink envelope with a pink ballerina on the front in the middle of the dinner table. Devin, Charisma's father, picked up the envelope and quietly read the note inside. He looked at Charisma, deep into her eyes, searching for something. One ounce of weakness in which he could argue the note he just read.

When Charisma noticed her father's stare, her heart continued to pound but even harder. But she knew to show no fear. She took a deep breath and looked right back at her father with the same intensity. When Devin saw the determination in his daughter's eyes that he knew was always there, he smiled at her. He placed his hand on his wife's arm and handed her the card with a small nod of acceptance.

His wife read:

Dear Mom and Dad,

I'm writing to you because my words don't seem to matter. I hope that once you read this you will finally accept my decision and give me your blessings to go to New York. Even if you don't, I'm sorry to say that I will have to go anyway.

I've been trying to tell you that I'm no longer the little ballerina (hence the envelope). I'm a woman now, and I'm ready to leave the nest. I have dreams and if I don't follow my dreams I will never wake up from my slumber. I will forever be walking in a cloud following the one in front of me to get to my destination.

It can't be that way...It won't be that way...I must make my own path...I must follow my heart. Most importantly, I must fulfill my dreams.

Love Always, Your Daughter,
Charisma

Before Lena took her eyes away from the letter, Charisma couldn't help but notice the tears forming in the corner of her eyes. When Lena finally looked up at Charisma, she realized just how hurt she was.

For the first time, she truly saw how badly her mother did not want her to go away. Charisma's heart broke to see her that way. She was even tempted to grab the letter from her hands and crumple it up as she hugged her and told her she would never leave her. But she also knew if she did it, there would never be another chance like the present. Instead, Charisma just sat there and watched as tears rolled down her face.

Lena looked at her husband for help, but he shook his head and whispered, "let her go, Lena. Just let her go."

Charisma thought this awkward moment would never end. Then suddenly, her mother stood up from the table, walked over to Charisma and just stood there for what seemed like eternity. Finally, Lena leaned down and kissed her daughter on the forehead and whispered, "may God be with you."

What was left of Charisma's heart shattered into pieces. With every ounce of strength she had, and without showing a glimpse of regret, she replied, "Thank you, Mother."

CHAPTER THREE
GRADUATION DAY

Graduation day finally arrived. Everyone in the auditorium was excited and rearing to go. Yet, Charisma couldn't help but remember the tears in her mother's eyes, realizing she could no longer hold on to her baby girl.

Charisma couldn't bear to imagine the sad scenario at the airport later that evening after her graduation dinner. She decided it was best to catch a flight to New York right after graduation. She would stay with her cousin until summer was over and the dorms opened up. She knew the longer she stayed, the harder it would be for her to leave. She wanted to make it easier on everyone.

"So, Charisma are you ready to finally walk across the stage?" Brandy whispered to Charisma as their principal was giving the "never give up on your future" speech.

"As ready as I'll ever be," Charisma whispered back without even looking at her.

When the principal finally called Charisma's name and she walked across the stage, she looked over to her mom and dad. She saw the eyes of two proud parents. All Charisma could think was "*if this makes them proud, wait until I really make it. I can't wait to see their faces then.*"

Charisma accepted her diploma; her mother snapped picture after picture after picture. Her cheeks felt like they were going to burst from smiling so hard. Even after the graduation, Lena continued to snap pictures as if this was the last time she was going to see her daughter.

That evening, the whole Hennings family got together to congratulate Charisma on the first chapter of her life. School was very important to the Hennings family. Everyone in the family was very educated in their own fields. Doctors, Lawyers, Schoolteachers - they saw no excuse for not receiving a decent education. Charisma knew she had a lot to live up to.

During her graduation dinner, everyone mingled and enjoyed themselves. Meanwhile, Devin took her aside into the garage which was like a second home to him.

"Have a seat, Charisma. I need to talk to you," her father said with much seriousness in his voice. Charisma took a seat on her father's work bench as she so often did as a child admiring her father while he worked.

She remembered how much she loved to watch as he started with a couple of pieces of plain lumber. Gradually, they would start to form into the most beautiful pieces of furniture she had ever seen. Being in her father's garage brought back so many wonderful memories between the two of them. Charisma always loved her father dearly. In the midst of remembering all the good old times, Charisma's father handed her a card which broke her trance.

"Don't open this until you are on the plane," he said. "But in the meantime, I need to talk to you about a few things. Listen, Charisma, I know you're a smart girl, but New York City is not the place for a girl like you. As much as your mother and I are against this, we know that as good parents, we need to let you go."

"Daddy, I'll be fine," she interrupted.

"Let me finish, Charisma. You're only 18 years old. Of course you would say that. You're invincible, I know," he said with mild sarcasm.

Charisma just shook her head but didn't dare interrupt her father again. She knew that as nice and wonderful as he was, he was not the one to mess with when he got upset. She had the pain etched in her brain from all the times she was spanked by him.

"Look, there are a lot of people there who live on the streets and know it like the back of their hands. Charisma, you're smart but you don't have street smarts and remember I told you that. As your father, I need to be honest with you. There are men who will lie to you to get anything they want out of you. If you even try to deny them what they want, they will take it. They will have no mercy on you. Do you understand me, Charisma?"

She just nodded her head and answered, "yes, dad." She was thinking to herself, "where does he think I'm going? He makes it sound like I'm going on a safari to the jungle or something. My goodness, my poor parents are really worrying about nothing. And *as for not having street smarts, I don't know about that. Smart is smart, books or streets. And I've got both."*

"I love you, Charisma," her father added. "You will always be my baby girl whether you like it or not."

Charisma stood up and hugged her father tight. She kissed him on the cheek and whispered, "I wouldn't have it any other way, daddy." While Devin hugged his daughter, he said a silent prayer and hoped that God heard him.

When they arrived at the airport later that evening, Charisma had already checked all her bags, received her boarding pass, and was ready to go. They were just waiting at the gate for the ticket agents to announce the boarding of her flight.

Everyone was quiet, even her best friend Brandy who had decided to come along to see her friend off. It was hard for Charisma to imagine life without her. Ironically, she was always there for her, seeing that their first meeting was a disaster.

Lena hadn't said a word the whole hour and a half ride to the airport. She just had this solemn look on her face. Even now, at the airport, she sat with her legs crossed kicking nervously, staring intently at the floor as if she had lost something.

Devin noticed his wife's nervousness. He put his hand lovingly on her leg as he whispered, "It's okay, Lena."

"You better write me!" Brandy playfully shouted at Charisma as the scenario in the airport was becoming too much for her to handle. Charisma had always been the emotional one. Brandy was never one for tears. So, whenever she felt an emotional button being pushed, she always played it off with sarcasm and jokes.

Charisma knew Brandy's game all too well. She pulled her close and hugged her tight as she told her friend, "I'll miss you too."

Brandy lost the battle with her tears as they rolled down her sculptured cheeks. "You know, if you're gonna miss me so much, you can stay right here and go to college with me," Brandy joked through her tears.

"*Spirit Airlines is boarding flight 1864 to LaGuardia. Again, flight 1864 to New York, LaGuardia is boarding at this time,*" a woman announced over the intercom.

"Well, honey, that would be you," Charisma's father playfully stated.

"Thanks, dad."

"Anytime, baby girl. Now come here and give me a big hug."

Charisma hugged her father as he whispered in her ear, "now, remember all I've told you. I know I should have taught you all this sooner, but I thought I was protecting you from something all this time. Now, I realize I may have hurt you."

"I'll be fine, daddy."

"I pray so, baby girl. I pray so."

Charisma walked over to her mother who was standing there with tears already flowing down her face. As she hugged her, she began to sob. Charisma was torn. No child should ever see their mother cry the way Charisma's mother was crying for her there in the airport.

"Why, Charisma?" Her mother questioned her. "Why do you find it necessary to leave your comfortable home, your loving family, and your best friend to go to God knows where for God knows what? What is it that you're looking for that you're so sure you can't find here?"

Charisma's mother was in full emotion. Tears were running down her bronze-colored face from all the tension, pain, and anger. She looked at her father for help. On cue, he gently took his wife into his arms as she sobbed profusely for her one and only daughter.

Charisma said a quiet "I love you" to her mother and headed down the jetway to the plane which would take her away. Away to her new life.

CHAPTER FOUR
NEW BEGINNINGS

"Dafney!" Charisma yelled out to her cousin as she struggled with her backpack full of some of her personal things.

"Charisma! I'm so glad you made it." A tall woman with mocha colored skin and hair pulled up into a high ponytail rushed over to Charisma. She grabbed her into a loving embrace.

As soon as Charisma was within a foot of her cousin, she could smell that sweet smelling perfume that she always wore. *Poison* by Christian Dior; that was her cousin's favorite perfume. She used to tell Charisma that it was called Poison because once men got a whiff of it, it would drop them to their knees begging for mercy.

Charisma's mother never liked her niece spending too much time alone with her. She didn't want Charisma to get any wild ideas from her. Of course, Lena loved her niece dearly, but she was young and always so free and wild. She was also very beautiful. But her beauty used to take her places that wouldn't get her anywhere fast.

Lena didn't exactly want Dafney as a role model for her daughter. She was even more cautious about the time they spent together when she began to notice how much Charisma's features resembled more and more of her nieces.

Every year, the older Charisma grew, the more everyone began to notice. Family members would always remark, "Oh you've got Dafney's high cheek bones" and "oh my goodness, look at those bold legs. Those are definitely Dafney's legs." And "what a beautiful head of hair just like Dafney's."

Lena was never jealous because her niece was very beautiful, and she was always proud of her. But she never wanted Charisma's beauty to get to her head like it did her niece.

Dafney allowed her looks to run her life and it got her into a lot of trouble through the years. Some troubles so serious that no one in the family ever spoke of them.

"I was beginning to worry about you. I almost pulled out my cell phone and called Lena."

"Please, don't do that," Charisma said sarcastically.

"Oh, I take it you had an emotional departure?"

"Emotional is not the word. They act like I'm running off to the jungle or something. It's only New York City! Big deal. You've lived here on your own for years and you're okay. Why is it that they think I can't make it here?"

"Well, Charisma, I am older than you. I've been there and done that and been back again. My whole time here was not peaches and cream. This can be a rough city, sweetie. Especially if you're new here and you don't know the ropes."

"Please don't tell me that my favorite cousin in the whole wide world is going to start acting like a parent!"

"Honey, I'm not trying to give you a long lecture," Dafney said. "As far as I'm concerned, we're roommates. I just happen to be your older, but let's not forget beautiful, cousin." Dafney joked as she took quick glances of herself in the windows of the airport lobby.

Charisma laughed as she watched her cousin admire herself. She noticed her cousin's eyes and saw the similarity that everyone in the family always talked about. They both had the same almond shaped eyes and high cheekbones.

Dafney noticed Charisma's stares and nervously asked, "okay, sweet, so is this all you brought with you to the Big Apple," pointing at her backpack.

"Are you kidding me?" Charisma blurted out, noticing her cousin's uneasiness. I've got luggage coming down the carousel, and my mom is sending the rest of my things with a truck later on."

"Well, let's get moving. Life waits for no man. Or should I say no woman," Dafney said with a slight wink to her baby cousin.

When they finally got to Dafney's Yukon Danali, Charisma's heart skipped a beat. She never knew too much about her cousin. For some reason, no one ever talked much about her, and she didn't visit often. But this vehicle was beautiful. Almost as beautiful as her cousin who she was beginning to admire more and more by the minute.

It had leather seats, a sunroof, a nice system, and a television on the back of each front seat. There was also a smell in the vehicle that she couldn't seem to put her finger on. It was a real strong smell; one that was beginning to make her head spin. But eventually, with all the excitement of being in New York, she forgot all about the smell and the headache it was giving her.

After Charisma leaned back into the soft leather to finally relax after her flight, she looked over at Dafney and noticed her jewelry. She wondered why she hadn't noticed them before; they were really nice. One hand had a diamond bracelet dangling solo on her wrist as she held on to the steering wheel. And the soft, but obviously expensive chain delicately sitting around her neck was a little hard to ignore.

Charisma was in a daze gazing at the beautiful jewelry and the expensive truck with all of its features. Dafney pulled her out of the trance like state when she said, "Charisma, I have to make a quick stop. I hope you don't mind."

"Please, I don't mind at all. The more of New York City that I get to see, the better for me."

Charisma was afraid that she'd spoken too soon when they pulled up in a sketchy area. The apartments were green and dingy, and nearly half of the windows were replaced with plywood. There wasn't even a square of green grass in sight. And she noticed that the people walking up and down the street were talking to themselves. One man was having a serious fight with himself. Another man, in ripped and tattered clothing, seemed to be peeing in a corner. Charisma became nervous. She held on to her backpack for dear life.

Dafney noticed her cousins' fears and giggled. "I take it you've never been to the projects before?"

"No, I can honestly say that I haven't."

"Well, there's a first time for everything. Don't worry, you're okay with me. I used to live around here, so they know me well."

"Here?!" Charisma shouted at her cousin in amazement and shock. "Why?" Dafney paused before answering her cousin's question. She thought about her answer, remembering her terrible past.

"I was real young and on my own. I had no job, nowhere to turn, and no one to turn to," she said as she stared off into space. "That is until I met a friend...a friend who came to my rescue."

"Hey Dafney, what you need today? You bring me a new customer," asked a slanky woman with very slurred speech. She was also missing three teeth right in the front of her mouth. She rushed to Dafney's window interrupting their conversation and also snapping Dafney back into the here and now.

"Naw Tina, 'dis my cousin, she ain't bout none a 'dis hea." Charisma was surprised to hear her cousin's change of accent. It was like she was two different people.

"Um, I need my usual and hurry. I'm not trying to get arrested up in hea. You know with my new rep and all, it won't look too good," she said with a smooth giggle.

Charisma saw the skinny lady, who looked like she hadn't combed her hair in days, hand Dafney something through the window. It looked like a small plastic bag. Dafney reached her hand out the window and handed the same lady some crumpled up money. Then, as quickly as the woman arrived, she was gone.

"Thanks for being so patient, hun. Let's be on our way home now," Dafney announced. Now, it was the upscale high-class Dafney again. It was as if nothing had just taken place.

Charisma felt like she was on some sort of hidden camera television show like the one her and her mother Lena used to watch together on Sunday nights. Something told her that she wouldn't have too many of those quiet nights sitting around watching television anymore. She was already beginning to feel a bit homesick.

When they finally pulled up to Dafney's townhouse, Charisma had pretty much regained her composure. The outside of the house was pretty plain, nothing much to look at, but still really nice.

As they walked inside, Dafney ran over to the phone, shouting behind her, "Go on and make yourself at home. Let me go check my messages!" Dafney yelled out and pointed Charisma in the direction of the living room, dropping her keys on the side table by the front door. Right next to the most simple but beautiful and cozy couch she had ever seen.

Charisma stood at the front door paralyzed. Never before had she seen anything like this townhouse. Of course, her house back in Florida was nice but it was homely. This place was out of MTV cribs. This was awesome!

She looked over in the direction that her cousin was pointing in. She noticed a bright, almost orange-looking, wall and right in front, a red leather couch with wooden arms. She slowly walked over to it and sat down. She rubbed her hands across the leather and thought to herself, "as beautiful as my fathers' furniture is, his pieces don't compare to these."

She looked up and before her was a sight that would have made any man cry. There was a balcony with very stylish rot iron furniture with yellow and blue pillows on them. But best of all was the view. There, over her cousin's balcony, was the Hudson river as big as an ocean. From a distance, you could see the statue of Liberty.

Charisma thought of how wonderful this spot would be to write her poetry. While she was gazing out into the water, Dafney yelled out to her.

"Go into the kitchen and grab yourself a coke. I'll be right out!" That's when she noticed the huge, spacious kitchen with yellow walls. It was across from the ivory grand piano that sat in its own spot surrounded by nothing but air and beauty.

She walked over to the kitchen, excited by all the color this apartment contained. It was like everything that had built up inside her all these years was splattered onto the furniture and the walls. All of her loneliness and wanting was right here in this apartment. On the walls...on the couch...in the furniture...it was all laid out right here in a beautiful rainbow of colors.

Charisma could barely contain her excitement! All she could think was, *"I'm going to live here! Oh my gosh!"* She was beaming with excitement when she heard a deep voice coming from the direction of her cousin's bedroom. She quickly realized it was the answering machine.

"Hi, baby, it's me just checking to see if you got the flowers I sent. Call me back. Love you." *Beep!*

Charisma looked over at the round glass dining table in front of the cobalt blue wall in the dining room. She noticed what looked like two dozen roses in a beautiful crystal vase sitting in the center of the table.

Then she heard another message. "Dafney, slight change in plans. We need you at 5:00 a.m. for tomorrow's shoot. Sorry about the short notice but you know how this business is. Be there and be ready for the camera." The voice sounded serious yet slightly playful. Charisma wondered what that was all about.

"Shit!" Charisma heard Dafney curse from her bedroom. She walked halfway down the hall and asked, "are you okay?"

"Yeah, I'm okay. Sorry about that. It's just that I had plans for us tomorrow. It's only your first day here and they've moved my photo shoot to the morning."

"Oh, I'll be fine. Go ahead, do your thing. Life waits for no woman, remember?"

"Ah, you catch on quick little Charisma."

"Please, I am not little. Remember, were roommates. I don't need you to babysit me," Charisma said, reminding her big cousin of her statement earlier in the car.

"Yes, you're right, roommates."

"Just one question, Dafney."

"Sure, what is it?"

Charisma walked inside her cousin's bedroom after standing in the doorway almost afraid to touch anything. Everything looked so fragile. She saw a huge picture of her cousin in a leopard print bikini on the wall over her bed. She couldn't help but notice her leopard print comforter that coincided perfectly with the picture.

The bed was huge; it had 4 wooded poles with jungle like carvings on each one. The walls in this room reminded her of the color of a lion. On the floor, in front of the bed, lay the most beautiful piece of carpet she had ever seen. It was white and fluffy. It almost looked like a white polar bear sitting curled up in front of the bed.

Dafney noticed her cousins' eyes gazing around the room and knew her question before she even asked it. She answered the unasked question. "I worked hard, Charisma, and I still work hard. Everything that I have did not come easily to me. I worked for it all."

Charisma understood her cousin and accepted her answer. But there was still something more that she wanted to know so she continued.

"I still have another question."

"What is it, sweet?"

"How... how can I have this?" Charisma asked Dafney as she opened her arms to the whole apartment.

Dafney's eyes widened in surprise from the forwardness of her little cousin. She was also impressed and hurt at the same time. She remembered her past. How she really got to where she is now and all the tears that she shed to make it to this place. She wondered was it all worth it.

Sure, her cousin was more than pretty enough to be a model. But was she strong enough to stand the downs that came along with all the perks of being a model? She wasn't sure what to say to her at that moment.

Then finally she asked, "How would you like to come with me to the shoot tomorrow morning? If you still like what you see, I'll set you up with my photographer."

Completely catching Dafney off guard, Charisma jumped on her cousin's bed and grabbed her into a big bear hug. She was so happy she forgot all about how careful she was trying to be to not break anything.

"Thank you, Cousin Dafney, thank you so much! You don't know how much this means to me!"

"Okay, Okay. One thing though," Dafney said trying to get some air through Charismas embrace.

"Anything!"

"The whole cousin Dafney thing has got to go. It sounds so hillbillyish."

"Oh, okay. Sure, I can handle that. So, what should I call you then?"

"Just plain out Dafney is fine with me...roomy.

CHAPTER FIVE
THE DECISION

That morning, Charisma was ready and rearing to go. She got up before Dafney and decided to make breakfast for the two of them. At home, Charisma's mother always made sure they had breakfast before they left the house. It became second nature to Charisma to make breakfast since her mother was not there to do it for her.

Proudly, she announced that breakfast was ready. Her cousin came rushing down the hall into the kitchen with the cutest little summer dress on and a pair of high-heeled, beige, strappy sandals to match. Again, her hair was up in a high ponytail, but this time wrapped around into a beautiful bun on top of her head. To top everything off, she was spraying her usual *'Poison'* on her pulse areas to knock them dead.

As she came around the corner and stepped into the kitchen, she looked at Charisma and pouted. "Oh, sweet, I should have told you I can't eat before a shoot. Much less this extravagant meal you've laid out here. She looked around in amazement at the spread and said, "Wow! It must have been Lena who taught you to cook like this!"

Charisma was so hyped up by that compliment. The fact that Dafney did not even take a bite of the eggs she slaved over did not phase her one bit.

Dafney grabbed her keys and Coach bag and asked, "are you ready?"

That's when Charisma began comparing herself and what she was wearing to her cousin and her ensemble. Dafney noticed Charisma's private self-ridicule and took her by the arm.

"Come on, sweetie, let's do a quick makeover."

They stepped into Dafney's huge walk-in closet. She pulled out a black knee length, almost business looking, skirt and a purple strappy top. She gave Charisma a pair of black Nine West sandals to put on. Dafney quickly went into her jewelry box that stood human size from floor to eye level. She pulled out a very dainty silver chain with a little ivory pendant hanging from the middle.

Dafney stepped back and looked at her little cousin. She was amazed at how much Charisma looked like her. It was truly almost like looking in the mirror. Dafney felt like she needed to step out of the room and get some air. She told Charisma she'd be waiting for her by the door.

Looking at herself in the mirror, Charisma felt proud. She felt more like her big cousin especially since she was wearing her clothes. She added her own finishing touches by pulling her hair up into a neat bun on top of her head.

"Well, if I'm going to look the part, I might as well act the part too," she thought to herself, looking in the mirror and trying to

find the right attitude for the day. In the middle of admiring herself, she heard Dafney call out. "Come on, Charisma, let's go! You look fine!"

As she gave herself one last glance, she noticed the round, red bottle of *Poison* on the dresser. She sprayed it on as she whispered, "let's knock 'em dead, girlfriend."

*****

As soon as they stepped onto the set, a tall handsome man with hazel eyes and soft olive colored skin rushed over to Dafney. He kissed her on the cheek while rubbing her shoulders. When he turned around, she noticed his thick dark ponytail hanging low in the nape of his neck.

"Dafney, darling, I'm so glad you got my message. This is a very important shoot. For you to miss it, that would have been it for your career."

Charisma noticed that this man spoke to her cousin almost as if he were her father. She also noticed that Dafney never really looked this man in the eyes. Her whole demeanor just sort of changed. From the short walk from the truck to where they now stood, her cousin was not the same person. It was like she was giving this man way too much respect.

"Franky, I want you to meet my little cousin Charisma. She's going to be staying with me for a while until she starts college after the summer is over."

"Ah, Charisma...what a name. It's so...how you say? Charismatic! You are a very beautiful girl," he said with a strong, French accent.

"Well, that's another thing I wanted to talk to you about. She is interested in what I do and wanted to sit in on this shoot. If she likes it, she wants to give it a try. What do you think, Franky?" She said in almost a begging tone.

In the middle of her sentence, he quickly held his palm up to Dafney's face silencing her. "Francois," he said to Charisma, holding out his other hand in the form of a formal introduction.

Charisma slowly took his hand and shook it. "Pleased to meet you, Francois." Even though, at that moment, she was really not so pleased.

First impressions are lasting, and her first impression of this Francois was not a very good one at all. She was almost afraid of him, and she didn't even know him. She could see why her cousin acted the way she did in his presence.

"Well, turn around. Let me take a look at you," he said curtly.

Charisma looked at her cousin for approval. Dafney gave her a quick nod, telling her to go ahead and do as he said.

"Nice, very nice! Young, perky, everything in place. Beautiful, very beautiful."

A clothing coordinator was walking past with a cart of all the swimsuits for that day. Francois stopped him, took off a white thong bikini, and sent the man on his way. He looked Charisma directly in the eyes and told her, "here, put this on so I can get a better look at you."

Charisma's knees almost fell out from beneath her. She glanced over at her cousin with fear, and he quickly snapped at her.

"Why do you keep looking at her?! Can't you just take the suit and put it on so I can get a good look at you? What's the problem here? You know what? Forget it. I really don't have time for kids. I deal with professionals and professionals only.

I was willing to give you a chance because you're Dafney's family. Do you have any idea how hard it is to get in the spot you're standing right now? I don't think you do."

With a quick change of tone, as if he were Dr. Jekyll and Mr. Hyde, he calmly looked at her cousin and said, "Dafney, be ready in 20 minutes. The sooner you're ready, the sooner we'll begin." Then, after taking one last look at Charisma, he very coolly strolled back over to the set as if nothing ever happened at all.

"Whew, he can be such an asshole sometimes. Come on, Charisma, let's go over to my dressing room."

"Who is he anyway?"

"Well, he's a little of everything. He's my agent. He takes some pictures of me. He runs all these shoots. He gets me great shoots all over the world and ...and he's a friend."

"A friend? That monster is a friend of yours?" Charisma asked in disbelief.

"Charisma, from what just happened out there, you really can't judge Franky. I mean, he's really a sweet guy."

"You mean Francois," Charisma said sarcastically.

"No, I mean Franky. He just did that for show, Charisma."

"And what about that string he wants me to put on?"

"Charisma, what do you think models wear? Especially when we do swimsuit shoots."

"Yeah, but come on, Dafney. I just met this man, and he expects me to put on dental floss and prance around in front of him."

"What about when you go to the beach, Charisma? You're not thinking about those men. What makes him so different? And he's willing to pay you and possibly make you famous when those jerks at the beach are there just to ooh and ahh at you!"

Charisma stopped and thought about it for a moment. She realized that she was being kind of ridiculous about the situation. How many times has she turned on the television or picked up a magazine just to find a beautiful woman in practically nothing draped across the front cover? Her cousin was also right about the beaches. Women do walk along the beach in barely anything and the men just sit around and drool. *"If you're going to wear a string anyway, modeling is a more respectable way to do so and get paid at the same time,"* she told herself.

"Charisma, I did tell you that there were a lot of downs to being a model. If you're not interested, I won't be upset at you. Don't you have a great writing career you're looking forward to? That *is* why you came over here to New York anyway, isn't it? Not to become a model."

Dafney was right. Charisma's dream was to become a famous African American writer/poet. That really was her reason for coming all this way. But on the other hand, Charisma had already been introduced to this life of expensive things. It was going to be hard for her to turn back now.

After seeing her cousin's gorgeous apartment and her huge Yukon SUV…Seeing all of her expensive jewelry, clothes, the furniture… How can she now go to a crowded dorm room and live a normal, simple, college life?

Charisma had tasted the forbidden fruit. Now she wanted the tree that it came from. The want was growing in her minute-by-minute, hour by hour. She felt that she had to make the decision to put her poetry to the side for now and see how far this modeling thing could take her.

She looked up at her cousin who was letting her hair down and getting ready for her photo shoot. She said, "Tell him to give me the string...I'll put it on."

CHAPTER SIX
RED FLAGS

"Wait in here and Franky will be right with you." A tall woman directed Charisma to a huge dressing room across from Dafney's with the initials F.D. on the door. She sat on the cold, black leather couch in the tiny thong bikini covered by a short white robe that barely covered her behind. Chills went up her spine. She was already cold sitting in that dressing room with barely anything on. With her nerves acting up on top of that, her teeth began to chatter.

Finally, there was a knock on the door and Charisma quickly stood up.

"No need to stand up just yet," Franky said as he walked into the dressing room. He waived at Charisma to sit back down without even looking in her direction. He went over to the bar and poured himself a glass of brandy with some ice. With his back still to Charisma, he asked, "would you like a drink?"

"No thank you...I don't drink."

He slowly turned around and faced Charisma. He looked her straight in her eyes and swallowed the drink that he had just fixed for himself in one gulp. All without taking his eyes off her once. He placed the glass down on the bar and walked over to where she sat. She began to shiver. Not because she was cold but because of the cold stare and presence of this man standing over her.

"So, you say you don't drink?"

"No sir, I don't," she managed to repeat herself.

"Where are you from again?"

"Florida."

"Well, I don't know how they do things in Florida, but here in the city we like to try things at least once. So, again, I ask you, would you like a drink?"

Charisma froze at the forwardness of this man. She could never imagine that someone could actually be this way. Yet she was too afraid to deny him his wishes a second time. She forced herself to answer with what he wanted to hear. "Yes, actually, I would like a little."

"Well now, I knew deep down you did. Let me fix you a small beginner's glass." He turned to Charisma with a small glass of the same brown drink that he had earlier and another for himself.

"Let's make a toast; a toast to a new friendship." They clinked glasses and as usual, in one gulp Franky's was done. Charisma tried to do the same and swallowed the whole thing. As soon as the drink hit her throat, she dropped the glass and fell back to the couch gagging and coughing.

Franky quickly rushed to the bar and poured her a glass of water. He helped her drink it all down as she gasped for air.

As the burning in her chest subsided, she looked over at Franky with embarrassment. She thanked him for the way he rushed to help her the way he did.

He gently rubbed her back and with a smile asked her, "what made you swallow that liquor down the way you did?"

"I saw you gulp yours down. I thought that's the way to do it."

"Yeah, but I can handle my liquor. This is your first time. You're a beginner and here you are taking shots like you're a sailor. What are you trying to do - kill yourself?"

When he noticed the embarrassed look on her face, he tried to lighten the moment by saying, "I'll bet you don't feel so cold anymore, now, do you?"

She admitted to him that she didn't and thought to herself, *"maybe he really isn't that bad. He just takes a while to get used to, that's all."*

"Well, whenever you're ready, I'm ready to get a good look at my new model." He sat back in his chair and put his foot up on the table.

Just hearing that made Charisma very excited. All of a sudden, she felt comfortable; like she'd known him for years. So comfortable that she jumped up to take off her robe. She must have stood up too quickly because she had a quick head rush and fell back down to the couch.

Franky let out a hearty laugh and got up from his chair. He rushed over to her, helping her up to her feet. He looked Charisma in her eyes and said, "let's try this again, but a little slower this time. Remember you're a beginner. You don't want to move too fast with that alcohol in your system. I would hate to see you fall and hurt that pretty little face of yours." He used the back of his hand to brush a couple strands of hair away from her face.

She was so overwhelmed by his touch and caring words that she stood without being asked again and looked deep into his eyes. She slowly took off her robe and let it fall freely to the floor.

Standing before him, a man she barely knew, with only a string and two triangles barely covering her body, she felt empowered! She slowly turned herself around.

With a smirk on his face, he motioned for her to put her robe back on. He saw what he needed and was satisfied.

"Nice. Very nice, Charisma. I want you to start this weekend. We have a photo shoot with Calvin Klein and a new designer coming out. I want you to do both."

As he was leaving the room, he passed by Charisma who was struggling with her robe. He took the laces into his hands and tied the knot for her. He pulled her chin up to face him and said, "now, I want you to tell Dafney to take you home. Get some rest, take a Tylenol, and drink plenty of water. You're going to have a serious hangover if you don't."

He kissed her on her forehead and said, "I'll see you this weekend. Be ready and look pretty for the camera." And then he was gone.

As quickly as it all happened, it was all over. Charisma was all tingly inside over this man that she just met. She could see how Dafney seemed to never want to disappoint him. How she just seemed to go along with whatever he said. His charm was just so powerful. Who could resist?

*****

On their way back home, Charisma lay back in the passenger seat fast asleep, dreaming of her new career. Of how long it would take her to get to where her cousin is now. Dafney looked over at her intoxicated little cousin and just shook her head, wondering if she was doing the right thing for her.

She remembered when she was in Charisma's shoes. When she had first met Francois. She remembered how afraid she was and how he intimidated her until she finally broke and gave into him. She remembered how he got her drunk and then tried to take care of her to make her feel like he really cared. She knew that he had done the same with Charisma.

She kept telling herself that she was doing the right thing for her little cousin. That all models go through this type of thing. That it's just obstacles that models need to get over to make it to the top. Luckily, Charisma has her to help her. Whereas, when she was Charisma's age starting off, she had no one. No one but Franky, and he knew it.

Looking over at her cousin, her mind wandered off to when she first met Franky.

"Darling, before we begin, I brought you a drink." Franky sashayed into the room that young Dafney was sitting in waiting for her turn to be before the camera. She'd heard about Franky through a friend while in college. Dafney was in college for graphic design when her world came crashing down and she lost her scholarship. She needed a new direction because she refused to go back home to her family for help.

"What's this?" She asked, taking the drink from his hands.

"Just a little something to loosen you up is all."

"I'm okay. I don't want anything to loosen me up. Can I just model and be on my way?"

Within a split second, before Dafney could even see it coming, Franky grabbed the glass from her. He threw it across the room causing it to hit the wall and shatter to the ground.

In complete shock, Dafney put her hand over her mouth not knowing what to do in that moment. She stood and stared in fright at the man standing before her.

Franky immediately noticed her frightened look and walked closer to console her. "Oh honey, did I scare you? I'm sorry," he said, bringing her in close and moving her hands down from in front of her mouth.

"Listen, I get irritated when I feel ungratefulness coming from people that I'm genuinely trying to help. All I want to do is help you. Do you believe me?"

Still in shock, Dafney nodded her head not knowing what to think of this man. He had been so nice to her up until this moment of the glass flying across the room. She hadn't seen any signs of anything like this from him and here he is now explaining himself. Maybe it was just a moment. Maybe he's right. Maybe she was being ungrateful.

As he caressed her hair and continued to calm her, Dafney began to feel safe again. Almost like that moment never happened.

When she could finally speak, she said, "If you don't mind, may I have another one of those drinks you offered me? I'm sorry I didn't appreciate your efforts earlier. Thank you for all your help getting me into this agency. I really appreciate you, Franky. I really do."

"Sure, I'll go grab you another drink. No biggie, hun." As he headed out the door to go fix her another drink, Franky stopped and turned to look at her. He said, "I'm sure there'll be plenty of times during our time together for you to show me your appreciation, Dafney. I'm sure of it.

HOOOONNNNNK!!!!!!

Dafney jumped when the car behind her honked, waking her from her daze. She got herself together, realizing she had been sitting at the green light holding up traffic. Pressing the gas, Dafney couldn't help but wonder if this was the right thing she was doing for her cousin as she glanced at her again. Only time will tell.

*****

When Charisma woke up the next morning, she had the worst headache that she had ever felt. She tried to stand up to go to the bathroom and remembered the incident in the dressing room where she stood up too fast. She decided to get up very slowly this time.

The apartment was very quiet, and she wondered where Dafney was. She looked in her bedroom and saw no sign of her there. Heading to the kitchen to get a drink of water, she noticed her cousin sitting outside on the balcony. Her feet were up on a cushion as she read Cosmopolitan magazine. She looked to be dressed comfortably in a little short set.

After all that happened the day before, Charisma thought twice about going out there and facing Dafney. But she took a chance and went anyway. She opened the sliding glass door dividing the living room from the balcony asking, "Would you like some company?"

"Oh, hi sweet. How are you feeling?"

"Actually, not all that good."

"Don't worry, you'll be okay. Just drink a lot of water and I've got some Tylenol in my bathroom cabinet. A hangover can be the worst feeling. Believe me, I know."

"You're not upset with me?" Charisma asked, shocked that Dafney was not reprimanding her for her bad choice.

"Upset with you? Charisma, you're 18 years old. You're an adult, your choices are your choices. We're roomies, remember? If you need me, I'm here for you but I'm not here to judge you.

Plus, I've known Franky for years. Actually, since I was pretty much your age and he's good people. He can play rough sometimes but there's always a reason for his madness. Sometimes he just likes to test you to see how far you'll go, or he just wants to see the type of person you are. I mean, come on, he got me to where I am so he can't be all that bad, you know what I'm saying. His bark is really bigger than his bite."

Charisma was glad to hear that Dafney had no hard feelings about Franky. She breathed a sigh of relief and leaned back in the seat, looking out at the water.

This is truly a beautiful view. I just can't wait until I can have all this for myself one day. Maybe Franky and I can live together in a beautiful penthouse overlooking the Peace River. He and I can come out here and he can hold me as we watch the sun set at night. These were Charisma's thoughts while looking out at the water and watching birds as they flew by.

"So, I heard that you got a job this weekend," Dafney said, breaking Charisma out of her private thoughts.

Startled, Charisma jumped. She looked at Dafney wondering if she could tell what she was daydreaming about.

"Are you okay?" Dafney asked of Charisma already knowing what was going through her head. She used to have the same thoughts and dreams of Franky too. Especially when she was as young as Charisma.

He was just a smooth operator. He knew how to talk to the ladies of all ages, especially when he wanted something from them. His mind games were unbeatable, so there was never any point in ever trying to get over on him.

"Yeah, I'm okay. I'm gonna go on in and get that Tylenol from your bathroom."

"Alright, sweetie, make sure you drink a lot of water too."

After taking the Tylenol, Charisma laid back down in her huge white bed that her cousin had set up for her. She was finally dozing off when Dafney came into the room stating that she was going for her morning jog and asked if she wanted anything. Charisma thanked her, but really, she just wanted to rest.

Maybe 30 minutes after she had dozed off, the doorbell rang. She yelled to the person on the other side that she was coming. When she finally made it to the door, she opened it without checking the peephole. On the other side, she found Franky standing there holding a single rose.

"Hello, Charisma. Is Dafney home?"

"No," Charisma replied as calmly as she could, seeing as how she was about to explode on the inside just from seeing his face again.

"Good, I'm here to see you anyway."

"Me? For what?"

"What? I can't pass by and check on how my new girl is doing?... I was concerned. Here, I brought you a rose."

Charisma thanked him and took the rose into the kitchen to put it into a glass.

"Can I come in?"

"Sure. Do you think that Dafney would mind?"

"Mind? Who do you think got her this apartment and paid for all the things in it?"

Charisma looked at him shocked and confused about why he was paying for her cousin's things.

"You bought all these things?" She questioned. "Why?"

"With a devilish smile on his face, Franky answered. "Let's just say that I like to take good care of the girls who work for me and... we're also really close friends if you know what I mean.

From that, Charisma knew exactly what he was trying to say. She felt so stupid wondering why she hadn't figured it out before.

"Dafney is sleeping with you?"

"Franky was very impressed by Charisma's forwardness and replied, "My, don't we catch on quickly?"

"So, she really didn't work hard for all these things, did she?"

"Well, I wouldn't exactly say that she didn't work hard..."

"Please! Charisma shouted before he could finish his comment. I don't need to know the details. Matter of fact, I really don't need to be here. You people are sick!" Charisma said, grabbing her shoes from the floor.

"Charisma, wait." Franky said calmly as he got up from the sofa and walked over to her. "It's not all that bad. Let me explain."

"No! Save your explanation for the next girl. I just want to get out of here and head over to my dorm," she shouted, backing away from him.

"Charisma, look around you. Wouldn't you like to have all these things that you see? "A nice car, nice clothes, a huge apartment, and an exquisite man," he added. He blocked her in, up against the sliding glass door of the balcony.

Charisma looked up into his hazel eyes filled with so many promises that she couldn't resist him. He was so close to her that she could smell his cologne. She could feel him breathing as he leaned up against her with his body. Her heart was pounding because she had never kissed a boy before much less a grown man, like Francois.

"I can give you all of this and make you famous, but only if you let me," he said to Charisma. He was so close to her face that they were sharing the same breath.

"He is so handsome," she thought to herself, trying to keep her composure.

Then he asked her, "will you let me? Will you let me give you all of this, Charisma?"

Without hesitation, she answered "yes," right into his mouth as he gently kissed the answer straight from her lips.

"I promise to take good care of you, Charisma," he whispered into her ears.

As she closed her eyes, she dropped her shoes back to the floor and let herself go into his arms.

CHAPTER SEVEN
OH, HOW NAÏVE!

"Charisma, I'm going to a party tonight. Do you want to come?"

"Sure, who's going to be there?" Charisma asked, hoping to hear Franky's name somewhere on the guest list.

Dafney caught on to her little cousin's efforts and answered, "No one that you would know. Just some of my friends who are putting on a bash."

Charisma was a little disappointed because it'd been days since she'd heard from Franky. On the other hand, she had never been to a real party before and wanted to go. She wanted to see what she was missing out on all these years that her parents kept her prisoner in her home, so she agreed.

"Great," Dafney said. And I've got us both dates.

"Dates? I don't need a date, Dafney. Thank you, but I'm okay."

Dafney knew that Charisma was already feeling committed to Franky. It was all part of his plan; she knew it all too well. She felt that this was the best time to talk to Charisma about Franky and his ways.

"Look, Charisma, let me explain something to you. This may be a little hard to understand but you have to learn to have some street smarts here. This is not the country; this is the city. New

York City. It has pity on no one. What I'm trying to say is - stop being so naive."

"Naive!" Charisma yelped.

"Calm down, Charisma. It's not necessarily a bad thing, but if you're not careful your innocence can get you or your feelings hurt. Look, let me just come right out with my point. Okay, look… people like Franky, for example, you can't allow your heart to get mixed up with him. You have to use him just the way he uses you."

"You mean the way he uses you!" Charisma said angrily. "I'm not the one sleeping with him!" Charisma could feel the blood rushing to her cheeks as tears threatened to fall from her eyes. She was emotional and hated it when this happened. She always wore her emotions on her sleeve.

"Look, Charisma, I know this is hard for you to hear so I understand your anger, but he's not using me, honey. At least not anymore. My heart isn't in it. I don't love him; I have a boyfriend. I used him to get me the good photo shoots. He gets me noticed and if you look around, he treats me quite well."

"You're disgusting, Dafney!" Charisma shouted. "I didn't know you could be so heartless. This poor guy is giving you everything, treating you with so many nice things, and you have the nerve to cheat on him!"

"Charisma, I don't expect you to understand everything right now, but you will eventually. As for me cheating on him, like I said, Franky is not my man. He knows that I have a boyfriend. He gets what he wants and he's happy. I get what I want and I'm happy."

"Charisma sat on her cousin's bed with tears swelling up in her eyes. She was full of confusion and hurt. She was wondering how she could be so stupid to think that this grown man could actually have feelings for her."

Dafney watched as her lil' cousin fought back tears. She sat down next to Charisma putting her hands to her face, bringing Charisma's face to hers.

"Listen, Charisma, I was once in your shoes. Believe me, I made a lot of mistakes, and I learned from each and every one of them. That's why I can pass what I've learned down to you. Maybe I should have never introduced you to Franky. But you seemed so interested in making it big and this is the fastest way that I know how. I mean, you can still do your college thing, but that wasn't for me. Do you understand what I'm saying? I was on my own and I had to make it somehow, and Franky was the best way for me. He's only one guy. It's not like it's a bunch of different guys and plus, he benefits me in so many ways."

"What about your boyfriend? How does he feel about all this?" Charisma asked her cousin through sniffles.

"He just thinks Franky is my photographer."

"So, what does Franky want from me?"

"Charisma, it's up to you. But you already know the answer. If you want to go ahead and do things the college way, go right ahead like I told you before. If you just want to model and take pictures and hope you'll get discovered, you can do that too. But it won't pay much, I'll tell you that. But let's not worry about that right now, sweets. We've got a party to go to tonight." Dafney tried to lighten the mood.

She got up to go take a shower and get ready for the night. She left Charisma sitting there on the tiger print bed confused and emotional.

That night, Charisma made a promise to herself. She would not let Franky take advantage of her the way he did with Dafney. She decided that she was going to become a model and have all the things that Dafney had without giving up her pride or her body. Then, after that, she would pursue her writing career and become a famous African American writer. She promised that if she saw Franky again it would be business and business only.

Charisma was focused, planning her next move. *"I can't stay here long. I know that much because if you're a good apple and you hang around with bad apples, you're likely to become spoiled, family or not,"* Charisma thought to herself.

"I'm just going to have to play her game for a while and use her for somewhere to stay until I find somewhere else." Charisma felt determined. She also felt hurt and betrayed. One of her most favorite people in the whole world turned out to be a slut, and she couldn't bear the thought anymore.

"Charisma, are you going to get ready?" Her cousin asked, coming out of the bathroom wearing a short pink robe on and drying her hair.

"Oh...yeah," Charisma answered a little taken back. She was so deep in thought she didn't even realize Dafney had gone to take a shower and was done already.

"Please don't tell me you're still stressing over Franky and his games," Dafney scolded Charisma with annoyance.

Charisma thought fast for a cool reply because she didn't want her cousin to know how she really felt about her now. How she no longer looked up to her the way she used to.

"Dafney, come on. I'm not sweating him anymore. You told me how he is and that's that. I'm just sitting here thinking about what I'm going to wear tonight. You know my wardrobe doesn't compare to yours," Charisma said, wondering if she had over done it.

"Sweetie, you don't have to worry about that. I'll lend you something nice to put on. Do you want me to have Franky take you shopping this weekend?" Dafney asked with a real upbeat tone.

"No!" Charisma blurted out. "I mean...no thanks," she said, trying to cover up her outburst. "I've got plans this weekend."

"Plans?" Dafney asked confused. "You don't know anyone here."

"I know, but I planned on going to visit the Statue of Liberty."

"Well then, I'll come with you," Dafney said, inviting herself along.

"Dafney, I'm okay. Remember, I'm not so little anymore. I just want to be alone this weekend and write some poetry," she lied to her cousin.

"Oh, okay. I can tell when I'm not wanted," Dafney said with a playful grin. "But wanted or not, were hanging out tonight and were gonna have a night filled with excitement. Right?"

"Ah...Right," Charisma answered slowly, afraid of what type of excitement her cousin had in store for her next.

CHAPTER EIGHT
LOOKS ARE DECEIVING

Walking up to the door, Charisma was so relieved to see that she was worrying all night over nothing. The house was beautiful, and the people walking in and out looked very decent. She figured it was just going to be a nice party with some of her cousin's model friends and their boyfriends, so she began to relax.

"Charisma, are you cold? Do you want my jacket?" Ivan, the guy that was her date for the evening, asked. She started to feel bad because since Ivan and Donald picked her and her cousin up from the house, she'd been a little cold toward them. She just wanted to protect herself from getting hurt anymore so she was trying to shut other people out.

But Ivan was beginning to open her doors again; he was just too nice for her to continue with her attitude. So, without a word to him, she took his hand in hers and they continued into the house. Ivan just smiled, feeling pleased to finally get some type of communication going with Charisma.

"Man, this party is really jumping!" Donald shouted over the music as they stepped into the house. Everyone was dancing and having a real good time. Charisma began to get excited.

"Donald, why don't you and Ivan go get Charisma and me a drink? We'll find somewhere to sit in this place."

"All right, honey, but I won't be long," Donald said as he gave Dafney a quick kiss on the lips. Ivan glanced over at Charisma, but she pretended not to notice.

"Come on, Charisma, let's find a nice spot for all of us to chill in this place." The deeper they walked into the house; the more Charisma noticed that some of the people there seemed to be moving a little slower than everyone else at the party. They almost looked like they were in a trance of some sort.

"What's wrong with them?" Charisma questioned her cousin.

"Nothing, their just on love."

"You mean *in* love, Dafney."

"No, *on* love. The love pill. You do know what the love pill is, don't you?"

Feeling a little embarrassed, Charisma admitted, "No, I'm sorry, I've never heard of it before."

Dafney thought to herself, *"My cousin has no clue about anything. What the heck were they teaching her over there in the country? It's amazing she made it this far without something happening to her."*

"Okay, let me explain. The love pill, also known as ecstasy, is just a little pill that makes you feel more relaxed, that's all."

"Then why do they call it the love pill?"

"Because when you take it, you just open up more to people and you show more love than you normally would."

"Is it a drug?" Charisma asked, cringing her face at Dafney.

"Not really, it just helps you to relax that's all," Dafney lied to Charisma. *"My cousin needs some sort of excitement in her life. Maybe this will be it,"* she thought to herself.

"We're back," Donald announced walking up with two drinks in each of their hands.

"What did you bring us?" Dafney asked excitedly.

"Oh, just a little Rum Punch for the ladies and a more manly drink for us gentleman," Donald said. Charisma was not looking forward to drinking again after the whole incident with Franky. She still had a little headache from that day.

"Here Charisma, I poured a little less for you. You don't seem to be much of a drinker," Ivan said, handing her a small glass of what looked like orange juice.

Charisma didn't want to disappoint Ivan, especially since he was so thoughtful, so she took the glass and thanked him. She took a little sip and noticed it tasted like punch, so she continued to sip some more.

"Whoa Charisma!" Ivan said quickly. "This is not juice," he told her, pulling the glass away from her mouth.

"Yeah, but it's so sweet."

Ivan was so impressed by her innocence that he took the glass from her and put it on the table next to them.

"Do you want to go outside and get some fresh air?"

"Sure, that would be nice," Charisma admitted, liking Ivan more and more by the minute.

"So, I hear that you moved here from Florida."

"Yeah, and I'm starting to wonder if I made the right choice."

"Why do you say that?" Ivan asked, noticing the troubled look on her face.

"I don't know. I guess things aren't what they seem to be around here."

"Well, I can see your point. You have to keep your guard up in the city at all times. Whereas in Florida things were pretty simple, right?"

"Right. Life here is just too complicated."

"You sound like you're giving up?"

"Even if I wanted to give up, I couldn't. I made such a big deal about coming here to my parents. I have to stay until I make something of myself. "

"Well, personally, I'm glad you feel that you have to stay. You know...for my sake," Ivan said with a little smile.

Charisma felt very special with Ivan. He was one of the first people that she felt really cared since she'd been here in this crazy city. Then, she smelled a familiar smell coming from inside the house. "What is that smell?" she asked.

"Oh, that's weed. You know, marijuana."

"That must have been what I was smelling in Dafney's car the other day."

"Most likely it was. Dafney can be a pot head sometimes from what I hear."

"I wonder if that was what she was buying when we went to that really bad neighborhood the other day."

"What?! Ivan shouted. How dare she take you with her to buy weed? Is she crazy? What if you guys would have gotten caught? Do you know you would have been arrested along with her just for simply being there? Promise me something, Charisma."

"What is it?"

"Promise me that you will be very careful where you go with your cousin and what you do. Family isn't always the best company. Do you feel me?" Ivan had such a serious look on his face. We know he asked the question.

"Actually," Charisma said slowly, "I was already starting to feel that way. Like Dafney was bad company."

"Well, she is, and you don't have to wonder anymore. Remember I told you."

"Thanks, Ivan. I really appreciate your advice."

"No problem. A pretty girl like you, alone in this city, needs some helpful hints." They stood there for a moment with the loud music from the party in the background and nothing really left to say.

Charisma glanced over at him trying to get a good look at his face. Earlier, when he and Donald came to pick them up for the party, she didn't care to notice what he looked like. She just wasn't interested in him then. She was only able to get a view of his profile, and she was very pleased so far.

He was tall and slim with a nice upper body; a clean-cut type of guy. He was dressed very nicely with a fresh, smooth haircut. The kind that made you want to rub the soft part on the back of his head. The top was a little longer with little curls and to top it all off, he had a smile to die for.

"What a beautiful night," Charisma said trying to fill in the silence.

"Not as beautiful as you," Ivan said, not missing a beat.

Charisma blushed as Ivan slowly walked over to her. He took her hands in his, leaned over to Charisma and gently kissed her on her lips. She closed her eyes savoring every moment of the kiss and hoped for many more.

"What do you say we go inside and see what excitement we've been missing out on?"

"I'm sure nothing as exciting as what's going on out here," Charisma dared herself to say but then felt real stupid once the words left her mouth.

Noticing her attempt at trying to say something cool, Ivan brought her close into a tight hug underneath the stars. Still holding her hand, he led her back into the house to rejoin her cousin and Donald.

"Charisma! Were you been cuz?" Dafney said, waving her hands around from the sofa where she was sitting.

Charisma walked over to Dafney and sat down. She was starting to tell her about the wonderful conversation she had outside with Ivan when she noticed something funny about her. Her eyes were tight, and her body was swaying uncontrollably from side to side.

"Dafney, are you alright?"

"Are you alright?" Dafney said, throwing the question back at Charisma.

"Dafney, seriously, you don't look so good."

"And you look beautiful." Dafney touched her cousin's face in such a loving manner. Look at these cheeks. Who wouldn't die to have high cheekbones like this? You're gorgeous, simply gorgeous."

"You're drunk!" Charisma proclaimed as she stood up and looked at Ivan for confirmation. "She's drunk!" She shouted and pointed accusingly at Dafney.

"Not exactly," Ivan uttered to Charisma unsure of what to tell her.

"From the look on Ivan's face, she knew that something was wrong. Then she remembered the people that she saw earlier that were moving real slow with a weird smile on their face. She looked over at Dafney and saw how her eyes seemed to be going in different directions and she couldn't sit still. Anything that came within her reach, she would stretch her hands out trying to touch it.

"It's that love pill! She took it, didn't she?" Charisma declared.

"Yeah, this is what drugs will do to you."

"But she said it wasn't a drug."

"Well, now you know better." Ivan said, staring at Dafney with no pity as she moved her arms about on the sofa to the music as if she were the tunes floating through the crowd.

"How could she do this to me? What am I supposed to do now?"

"I would leave her right there."

"Are you crazy? I can't leave her here. She's my cousin!" Charisma expressed to Ivan.

"Come on Dafney, we're going home." Charisma said, trying to lift Dafney from the sofa.

"Home? No! What are you talking about? The party has just begun." Dafney slouched back down deep into the sofa with her head falling backwards.

"Dafney, please don't do this to me," Charisma begged.

"Charisma, here are the house keys. Go home before you ruin my high." Charisma's heart skipped a beat. Her mouth fell wide open as she looked over at Ivan who just gave her an "I told you so" look.

"I'm not leaving her. Where's Donald?"

"You're fighting a lost cause," Ivan shouted as Charisma ran up the stairs in search of Donald.

"Just keep an eye on Dafney!" She shouted back.

Walking through the hallway on the second floor, Charisma heard lots of moans and groans coming from all directions. She knocked on the doors, whispering, "Donald, are you in there?"

On her way back down the hall, heading downstairs, she glanced over in the direction of one of the guest bathrooms and saw it ajar. She slowly walked over to it and caught a glimpse of Donald. She pushed the door open to tell him about Dafney. What she saw caused her to scream so loud that Ivan came running up the stairs.

When Ivan arrived at the bathroom door, what he saw froze him in his stance. There, sitting on the top of the toilet seat, his head leaning up against the bathroom wall, his mouth wide open with a brown belt tied tightly around his arm, and the needle still stuck in it...was Donald.

"Is he dead?! Is he dead?!" Charisma shouted to Ivan.
Realizing that Charisma was staring at the dead body, Ivan snapped out of it and quickly pulled himself together. He pulled

Charisma into his arms, covering her eyes away from the terrible scene.

"It's okay, sweetie. It's okay. Everything is going to be alright," Ivan said talking into Charisma's hair as she wailed and sobbed into his arms.

When the police and ambulance finally arrived and took Donald's lifeless body away in a brown body bag, Charisma just stared on from the police car shaking her head in disbelief. *"All of this must be a bad dream,"* she whispered to herself.

She watched the paramedics place her cousin on a stretcher and try to strap her down. From where she sat, she could see they were having a hard time. Dafney kept waving her hands around in the air telling them how wonderful they were and thanking them for all their help. She was smiling and laughing at nothing in particular, with no clue of the seriousness of the night.

She also watched the police arrest some people, frisk them down, and take things out of their pockets. One guy had a clear zip lock bag with what looked like little purple pills that the police officer took out of the front of his pants. Another had what looked like three or four tiny zip lock bags filled with a dark green almost grassy looking thing.

Charisma was astonished to see the type of people that were being arrested that night. These people all looked very decent and clean cut. No one even came close to looking like a thug.

Charisma was even impressed with Donald when she first met him. He was wearing a casual suit with a nice tie and very expensive shoes. She thought he had great taste.

Now look at him…He's dead. Looks are deceiving and crime has no color, style, gender, or class.

Charisma said to herself, *"This is one of the first, of many lessons, that I will take with me through life."*

She sat in the backseat of the dark police car watching all the commotion. The red and blue lights from their cars flickered through the clear night sky replacing the twinkle of the stars that should have been shining instead.

CHAPTER NINE
LIFESTYLE OF THE RICH AND FAMOUS

"Dafney, you've got to get up and do something with yourself!" Charisma shouted through the closed door of her cousin's room.

"Dafney! Do you hear me in there? It's been three months already since Donald passed away. You can't continue to lock yourself away from the world like this."

When Charisma received no reply from her cousin, she angrily walked away from the door and into the living room of the once beautiful apartment that she loved so much. She looked around the apartment and was disgusted. Clothes were on the sofa, dishes piled up in the sink, shoes thrown around with the match nowhere to be found.

Charisma immediately became upset. Before she would leave the house, she would always clean up. She'd wash the dishes and straighten up the entire apartment but by the time she returned home, the house would be a mess again.

As she cleaned the apartment again, Charisma tried to tell herself that her cousin was having a rough time right now and would soon snap out of it. She finished washing the dishes and was heading to the living room to pick up the clothes that were lying on the sofa and the floor. By the time she gathered all the clothes and threw them in the hamper she was so tired that she sank into the sofa to finally get some rest.

As she took a sigh of relief and found a comfortable position, she noticed some white powder on the glass coffee table before her. On the floor was a small razor blade. Charisma jumped up from the sofa, grabbed the razor, and headed angrily toward Dafney's room. Without even knocking, she pushed the door open screaming and yelling at Dafney.

"You just don't get it do you?! Do you, Dafney? It just wasn't enough that your own boyfriend died from this shit, but now you want to kill yourself, too? Look at me! Look at this!" She hollered at Dafney, holding the blade between her two fingers, waving it in the air.

"What do you want from me?" Dafney said slowly as she turned to face her irate cousin. "It's my life, Charisma. I'll do what I want with it. And this is my apartment, I'll do what I choose in it." She spoke very calmly as if the commotion that Charisma was causing was unnecessary.

"Have you seriously lost every piece of common sense that you had left?" Charisma asked her cousin.

"Look, Charisma, why don't you go back out, close the door, and leave me alone. You have a lot of photo shoots to worry about. You've got your little boyfriend now; go enjoy your little life and let me enjoy mine."

"Enjoy yours?" She questioned, feeling her temper rise even more. "You call this enjoying life? Look at this room, Dafney! Look at these clothes everywhere. When is the last time you've done laundry?"

"Charisma, I am an adult. The way I choose to live my life is my choice and my business, not yours."

"It is mine when I find your boyfriend dead in a bathroom of a drug party with a needle stuck up his arm!"

"You know what, you're really starting to get on my nerves," Dafney said with slow annoyance in her voice.

"Well, you know what? You've been getting on my nerves. I've just been polite enough not to say anything about it. Going around sleeping with Tom, Dick, and Harry. And for what? To get noticed? To have a few luxuries? You could have had that anyway on your own, without losing yourself and your dignity, had you been patient and worked for it. Now you sitting around on your ass all day and all night looking like a damn crack feign living for your next high! Oh, but wait, stay right there. Let me go get Robin Leech 'cause you living the life of the rich and famous."

Dafney jumped from her bed so abruptly that Charisma didn't even have time to think. She dashed for her little cousin and slapped her straight across the face.

"You better be careful how you talk to me, Charisma! You have no clue who I am!" And then without another word, she turned around and casually walked back to bed leaving Charisma standing there stunned.

As Charisma headed out of the bedroom feeling defeated, she made one last statement to her dear cousin. "Oh, by the way, as for me not having any clue who you are - you're right. But I know who you were. You were once the person I looked up to despite what anyone else thought. You were once the most beautiful woman in the world to me. Now, you're nothing but a junky."

Charisma left her harsh words to linger in the room with her cousin as she closed the door behind her and headed outside. She picked up the phone and called her now boyfriend, Ivan, to come pick her up from this hellhole, as she often described her recent living conditions. She grabbed her jacket to go wait for him downstairs, avoiding any more incidents with her cousin.

CHAPTER TEN
THE SURPRISE GUEST

"For the last time, why don't you move in with me?" Ivan asked of Charisma.

"I can't, Ivan. She needs me."

"Charisma, she needs you like she needs another high! When will you understand? What else does she have to say for you to realize that you can't help her? Honey, I know you feel like you need to take care of her and help her, but she won't even help herself. The only thing that will happen is that she'll bring you down with her. Charisma, you don't need to be around people like that, family or not. It's not healthy for you." Ivan looked up at the ceiling, stroking Charisma's arm as they lay in the king-size bed in his bedroom.

Charisma felt so safe with Ivan. They'd only been together four months and she couldn't imagine life without him. She lay there on his chest listening to his heartbeat and feeling the rise and fall of his chest. His breathing lulled her to sleep as it so often did. Besides all that's happened since she's been in this dreaded city, she was grateful to have met a guy like Ivan. He was nothing like any other guy, and at times, she felt like he was her guardian angel.

With her little knowledge of men, sex, and life in general, Ivan never took advantage of her. They've never had sex once, all the nights she's spent at his apartment. Not that she was complaining, but she was curious about why he hadn't made that move toward her. So, she asked him. Come to find out, he was still a virgin also and was waiting for the right girl and right time to come along. Charisma was pleased with the answer and left it at that.

The next morning Charisma woke up to find that Ivan had left for work already. She got up and put on her sweatsuit that was in her personal drawer. Ivan created one for her for all the nights she spent with him. She headed out for her morning jog. One good habit that she'd learned from Dafney.

She was standing in front of Ivan's dresser mirror, pulling her sweatshirt over her head, when she felt like someone was watching her. She quickly pulled the sweatsuit down covering her black sports bra. She pulled her hair away from her face to find that her instincts were correct. As she stood there before the mirror, she could see the image of a man standing behind her. She leaped around and screamed in terror.

"No, wait!" The man shouted, holding his hands up in the air. "I live here. I'm Ivan's roommate. I'm sorry for watching you get dressed. I just didn't know who you were and…

"Ivan never mentioned a roommate before!" Charisma blurted out, cutting him off and feeling unsure of him and his story.

"I don't know why; I was only gone for a couple of months. I went on vacation to see some of my family for the summer."

"How did you get in here?" She questioned him.

"I have a key," he said, holding up a set of keys before her. "You can call him on his cell phone if you don't believe me. I'll give you the number."

"I know the number!" Charisma snapped at him as she picked up the phone in the bedroom and called Ivan at work.

"Yes, may I please speak to Ivan Montgomery?" She asked the lady who answered the phone.

"Ivan speaking."

"Ivan, why is there a man standing here in this apartment with me, at this very moment, stating that he lives here?"

"What?! Jamal came back?!"

"Jamal?!" Charisma shouted into the phone realizing she hadn't even known his name. "Why is it that I have never heard about this Jamal before now?!"

"Honey, calm down. I didn't expect him to come back. No one knew when he left, and it's been a couple of months, so I just assumed he wasn't coming back."

As Charisma glanced up at him, she noticed he was eyeing her with a mocking grin on his face. The same way she had caught him eyeing her when she was standing in front of the mirror getting dressed.

Charisma instantly became enraged and told Ivan, "You know what? Maybe next time you should try not assuming because you make an <u>ass</u> out of <u>u</u> and <u>me</u>."

"Charisma, I'm sorry. I didn't know," Ivan pleaded.

"And I'll bet you still expect me to move in here with you, don't you?"

"Charisma, Jamal's harmless."

"That's beside the point, Ivan." Charisma whispered, even though Jamal had walked away into the kitchen. "Look, I'm going to have to think about it some more. I just don't know, Ivan. He gives me the creeps."

"Will you be there when I get home tonight?"

"How about I go back to my cousin's place, and you come by, and we'll talk?"

"Sounds fair enough. I'll pick you up after I get off. I miss you and I'm always thinking about you, Charisma. I just wanted you to know that."

Charisma felt so good inside hearing those words that she had already made up her mind about moving in with Ivan. As soon as she hung up the phone she headed out for her run, not wanting to spend any more time alone with Jamal.

On her way out the door she heard Jamal say, "So, I take it you're going to be our new roommate." When she turned around to face him, he was lying on the sofa, feet up and all, staring at the television.

"Well, you took it wrong. If anything, I'll be Ivan's roommate, not yours."

"Well, in this house, Ivan and I share everything." Jamal responded to Charisma without even taking his eyes off the television screen.

"And what is that supposed to mean!" Charisma demanded.

Jamal just continued to lie there on the sofa changing channels as if no one were talking to him. Moreso, as if he weren't talking to her in the first place.

She decided to ignore his rude remark. What she couldn't ignore was the chill that ran down her back when Jamal suddenly turned around. He devilishly smiled at her before turning back to face the television. She gathered her things and was out the door hoping to never have another encounter with this creep ever again.

CHAPTER ELEVEN
THE LETTER

During her jog, she thought about her parents. She started to feel guilty because she hadn't called them since she arrived in New York. She was not ready to face her parents with her new decision to follow a modeling career instead of going to college like they had planned for her.

She followed her heart and jogged to the nearest pay phone. Using her calling card, she dialed her old phone number.

"Hello," her father, Devin, answered the phone.

"Daddy...It's me, Charisma."

"Charisma?... Charisma! Where've you been?"

"Daddy, I'm sorry I didn't call but...

"No, I'm sorry Charisma. I should have never sprung that on you the way I did. It's just that I felt you oughta know by now. I'm so sorry, honey. Please don't be mad at Dafney. She didn't know any better; at the time she was very young..."

Charisma interrupted her father. "Daddy, what are you talking about? Why would I be mad at Dafney? What didn't she know?" Charisma questioned her father, not really surprised at affiliating Dafney's name with bad news.

"You mean...you don't know what I'm talking about? You never read the letter? That's not why you haven't called us all this time?"

"Well, daddy, that's what I was meaning to talk to you about," Charisma stated, forgetting all about her father's babbling about Dafney. Nothing that concerned Dafney really interested her at the moment anyway.

"What is it honey? Are you having trouble with your classes?" Devin asked, happy to change the subject.

"No, daddy. I'm...not exactly taking any classes at the time."

"What happened? Are they trying to tell you that the classes are full? Because I can call them up right now. They know you pre-registered, so they'd better find room for you in that class."

"Daddy, stop. It's not that. I'm sure they have plenty of room. I'm just not going right now."

"What are you telling me, Charisma?"

Charisma started trembling outside at the pay phone. She was hundreds of miles away from her father but was terrified. She had never been so disobedient to her parents. Up to now, she promised her parents she was going to New York City to attend college and pursue a writing career. Instead, she ended up not doing any of that and taking up a modeling career in the place of college.

"Yeah, they would be proud," Charisma said to herself sarcastically.

She decided not to tell her father about her modeling career just yet. She figured he wouldn't be able to handle it, and she didn't want to be responsible for her father having a heart attack.

"Daddy, other things came up."

"What could possibly be more important than your college career?"

"A modeling career," she thought to herself. She wouldn't dare say that out loud in fear that her father might just come through the phone.

"I knew I should have never agreed to you running off to New York. But I believed in you, Charisma."

Those words hurt so badly that they brought tears to her eyes.

"Daddy, I never said that I wasn't going. I just said not right now."

"Honey, do you have any idea how many people say they're going back to college and never do?" Devin asked his daughter.

"But I'm different, daddy. I know I'll go back; I have plans."

"I hope so, baby girl. You can't make anything of your future without a plan."

"Don't worry, daddy. I'll make you proud. Is mom in?"

"No, lately she's been staying late after school grading papers. I'll tell her that you called. Does Dafney have a number where we can reach you?"

"Well, I'm going to be getting my own line soon. I'll call you with the number as soon as I get it." Charisma lied to her father, not really ready for them to have a number for her. Especially since she wasn't sure where she was going to be staying.

"Alright, baby girl. But are you sure you're okay?"

"Positive, daddy. No need to worry. I love you and tell mom that I'll call her soon, and that I love her as well."

When Charisma hung up the phone, she let out a sigh of relief. Relieved to finally get that off of her chest, and to let her parents know that she was safe.

She continued on with her jog, enjoying the cool afternoon air. She was getting tired and decided to take a rest on a park bench that she spotted ahead right in front of the water. She figured it would be a great spot to think of some new poems and keep her promise to her father.

When she finally reached the bench, she noticed that the air was a little nippier than when she was jogging. She took her jacket from around her waist and put it on. She put her hands in the pocket of the jacket to warm her fingers.

She felt something like paper in her front pocket. Pulling it out, she remembered it was the letter her father had given her in the garage. He asked her not to open it until she got on the plane. All this time, she had forgotten about it. Charisma excitedly opened the envelope that had her name written across the front and read the letter from her father.

Charisma,

I'm not quite sure if this is the right way of telling you this. I know it will come as a complete shock to you, but it's about time you knew the truth. Despite what everyone else thinks, I can no longer keep this secret from you. You're getting older and you have the right to know. All these years that you've been with us, you've been my little girl and you've known me as your father, but I must tell you the truth. I am not your real father and the woman you knew to always be your mother is not your birth mother.

I'm sorry for this shock and if I could, I would take it all back, but I can't. I must move forward and tell you everything.

The one you have known, all these years, as your cousin is your real mother. Please don't be upset with Dafney. She was young;

she didn't know what else to do. I think she made the right decision by coming to us with you.

I am so happy to have been a part of your life. Every day with you has been a wonderful treasure for Lena and me. We've always loved you and treated you just like you were our own, but deep down we knew you really weren't.

Charisma, you can't imagine what it's like to look someone you love in the eye and lie to them every day. That's what we were doing to you, and I refuse to do it any longer.

I hope you can start a relationship with your real mother. Give her a chance, she's had a tough life. I hope you can understand the choice she made was not a selfish one. She did it for you. So you could have a better life.

I'm sorry to tell you this way. I guess I'm not the man I always thought I was. If I were, I would have had the courage to tell you something as important as this to your face, and not be such a coward and put it on paper.

Anyway, I must let you go now. Please be careful in that city. Remember I'll always love you, and no matter what you'll always be my baby girl.

Love,
Daddy

CHAPTER TWELVE
HONOR THY MOTHER

"Young lady, are you alright?" A little old lady asked as she was passing by with her two dogs and saw Charisma crying.

"Uh...Excuse me?" Charisma asked, looking up at the old lady startled and not sure of where she was for a moment. She was so focused on her father's letter that she didn't even realize that she was sitting there on the park bench crying in public.

"Are you alright?" The old lady asked again.

"Oh...Uh...Yes, thank you. I... I'll be fine." Charisma wiped her eyes and tried to pull herself together.

As the old lady moved on, Charisma stared in her direction clutching the letter in her hands unsure of what to do next. She knew she wanted to scream. Yell at someone. But who? There were so many people. So many people who have been lying to her… her whole life. The whole family was a conspiracy.

Charisma began to feel burning in her chest. She knew she was going to break down soon. She couldn't let it happen here, not in public with people passing by. But if not here, then where? She had nowhere to go. No one to run to. She needed some place to go and cry out the anger she felt inside.

Her cousin, now mother, is at the house that she would go to, but she's probably getting high again, so she couldn't go there. She would love to run to her boyfriend and talk to him, but he's at work. She could go to his house and wait there for him and have a good cry, but Jamal is there. There was no way that she was going to be alone in a house with that creep.

"What am I going to do?" Charisma said, putting her hands over her face. "My mother is a model/drug addict who practically prostitutes herself to get the things that she wants. She has no respect for herself much less for me and I'm supposed to be her daughter?"

"Who am I? Who will I become? The apple doesn't fall far from the tree. Isn't that the old saying? So, does that mean I'm going to grow up to drink, smoke, and do drugs? I have so many plans for my future. That can't be it for me! It just can't! I don't want to be like her! Please God, please don't let me be like her!" Charisma cried.

"I need to confront her. I've got to do it sooner or later so I might as well do it now." Charisma headed back to the pay phone from where she called her father and nervously dialed Dafney's phone number.

"Hello?" Dafney answered in a raspy voice.

"How could you do it?" Charisma painfully asked.

"Do what, Charisma? What are you exaggerating about now?" Dafney asked, already annoyed by the conversation.

"Exaggerating? You call finding out that my cousin is really my mother exaggerating?! How could you, Dafney? How could you give up your own child and then lie to me all these years!"

"Charisma wait..."

"No! You wait!" Charisma screamed into the pay phone. "How dare you lie to me all these years. How dare you?!"

"I had no choi..."

"Don't say it! Don't you dare say it! We all have a choice! You just made the wrong ones and now I have to suffer for your mistakes!!"

"That's what I'm trying to say. I didn't want you to suffer, Charisma. That's why I did what I did. I wanted the best for you."

"Why'd you really do it, Dafney? Why'd you really give up your own child? Oh, don't bother. Let me answer for you. It's kind of hard to get high and enjoy it with a screaming child on your shoulder, isn't it?" Charisma said scornfully.

"Charisma, listen to me!" Dafney yelled into the phone trying helplessly to defend herself.

"Listen to you? Oh, she wants me to listen to her. Isn't this ironic? My mother demands my attention," Charisma mocked.

"I wanted to tell you. I tried to tell you, but they wouldn't let me. They barely even let me see you."

"Oh, let me guess. Maybe because you're a crack head!" Charisma shouted sarcastically. "Look, enough of this back-and-forth bullshit. I'm on my way to pick up my things and I'm moving out. You can stay locked up in that room of yours when I get there, like you've been doing for the past 3 months because I don't want to see you. Matter of fact, I don't want to see or hear from you ever again." And then she hung up the phone.

Charisma waived her hands at the cabs on the street hoping that one of them would stop. Without any effort at all, a man with long black locks and a red, green, and gold hat pulled over to the curb.

"Where ya' headin', sweet girl." The cab driver said in a heavy Jamaican accent.

Charisma gave him the address to her cousin's, now mother's, house. She climbed in the backseat and cried her heart out. The driver couldn't help hearing her cries coming from the back seat. Looking through the rearview mirror, he saw a distraught young girl with bloodshot eyes crying like it was the end of the world.

"It can't be that bad, mi dear," the driver kindly said to Charisma.

"Believe me, it is."

"Did you take it to Him?" The cab driver asked Charisma.

Confused, she asked, "Take what to who?"

"Your problem. Did you take it to the Lord?"

Charisma just sat and looked at the man in disbelief. She hadn't heard anyone in the city even mention God much less talk to other people about Him.

"I'm not sure I understand," she said to the cab driver, wiping her eyes.

"What's there not to understand? You said your problem is that bad. Obviously, you must not have taken it to the Lord, because you wouldn't be looking the way you are right now. There's no problem too big for my God. Whatever troubles come your way, you hand it to Him and He takes over from there."

Charisma didn't say anything to him. She just leaned back in the old leather of the cab and thought about his words. He saw that she had stopped crying and asked, "Didn't your parents teach you this?"

"That's the problem. I found out that my parents are not really my parents after all."

"Oh, come on. Did they not feed you, clothe you, put a roof over your head, and send you to school every day?"

"Yes...but..."

"Then, they're your parents," he said, not letting her finish her statement. "Listen, child, it doesn't matter who gives birth to you. What matters is the one that takes care of you. The one that loves you and has been there for you. But remember, they might be your parents, but you have only one true Father and you always put Him first and that's the Lord God Almighty. He is above your birth mother and your caregivers."

They arrived at Dafney's apartment and Charisma got out. She reached through the passenger window to pay the cab driver, but he shook his head and said, "No, honey, it's free this time. You take care."

As she thanked him, she turned and headed toward the door of the building. But then she heard him call out her name, freezing her in her tracks.

"Charisma, one more thing. The woman who gave birth to you was only a carrier. She doesn't make you who you are, so don't feel destined to become who she is. You are who you make yourself out to be, and that's a special young lady."

When Charisma finally turned around to ask him how he knew her name, he was gone. The cab nor the driver were anywhere in sight and there was no sign of a car driving off. But for some reason, Charisma wasn't afraid. She felt a sense of peace fall over her and she walked up to that apartment with new direction.

CHAPTER THIRTEEN
WORDS ARE POWERFUL

"Dafney...Dafney, it's me," Charisma announced throwing her jacket on the sofa after entering the apartment.

"You're not going to believe what just happened to me." She shouted, pouring apple juice from the refrigerator.

"Dafney, are you listening to me?" She yelled, heading towards Dafney's bedroom.

"Oh, come on! So, what, you're not talking to me now?" Charisma asked, still talking through Dafney's bedroom door.

"I should be the one not talking to you. But if you'd let me tell you what just happened to me, you'd understand why I had a change of heart. Dafney, come on, let me in. Let's talk." Charisma pleaded while turning the knob. When she walked into the room, she found it in more disarray than before she left.

"Damn, this a mess. What the heck were you looking for up in here? I sure hope you found it," Charisma said, stepping over things to get to where Dafney lay on the bed.

"Dafney, you sleep? You didn't hear a word of anything I said, did you?" A chill went down Charisma's back all of a sudden. Instantly, she knew something was wrong.

"Dafney? Dafney, are you okay?" She whispered, gently shaking her trying to get her attention. When she received no answer again from her, she was sure something wasn't right. Even in a high or drunken state, Dafney would answer her or at least say something foolish.

As she stared very intently at Dafney peacefully lying in the bed, she slowly walked around to the other side of the room. She turned on the lamp on the side of the bed and noticed a memo pad with some writing on it. She quietly sat down on the edge of the bed so as not to wake Dafney, and nosily began to read the writings.

Charisma:

Do you know why I gave you that name?... Because I knew you were going to be a strong, sassy, and charismatic little girl. I knew you were never gonna back down from no one. You were gonna be that special one, and you are. I knew this from when you were in my belly. From your kicks and motions, I knew you were a fighter. I'm glad to see that my intuitions were correct.

Sweetie, I wanted to tell you who I was. But they felt as though it was best for you not to know. And that it was also best for you that I didn't see you often either. They figured you would have caught on seeing how we look so much alike and all.

I always loved you, Charisma. Letting you go was the hardest thing I've ever had to do, but the best thing...that I could do for you.

What was I supposed to do with you at 15 years old? I was a baby having a baby. Look how beautiful you turned out. If you were to be with me, who knows what you would be right now. I love you too much for that fate. I had already made the mistake of getting pregnant. I didn't know any better, but I don't believe in killing no child. I don't believe in that not one bit.

So, I went ahead and gave birth to you. But I was able to fix my mistake by giving you a better life. I hope this is making some kind of sense to you now. If not, I'm sorry. There isn't much more I can say but I love you.

I have and will be with you always.... Mommy.

Charisma lay down on the bed next to Dafney and put her arm around her.

"I love you too, mom. I'm sorry for everything I said earlier," Charisma uttered to Dafney through her tears. When she leaned in closer to Dafney, she felt something hard in the bed. She pushed aside the comforter to find an empty bottle of pills lying there in the bed.

As she jumped up, her heart instantly began to pound. She could immediately feel the force of her blood as it rapidly pumped through her veins. She turned Dafney over on her back and shouted her name over and over, frantically shaking her.

"Dafney?... Dafney!... No! You can't do this to me. Dafney, wake up! You're sleeping. I know you're sleeping, wake up!" Charisma yelled at Dafney, continuously shaking her.

"Why?" she cried. "You didn't have to do this. I would have loved you anyway," Charisma said, crying over Dafney's face.

"I didn't mean those things I said! They were only words! They were only words. Wake up!" She screamed and sobbed at Dafney, now holding her face in her hands. When Charisma finally realized that she would never get an answer from Dafney, she submissively laid her head on her chest and wailed.

She cried for anger. She cried for hate. Most importantly, she cried for love. For the love of her mother.

"You should have given it to Him...You should have given it all to Him," Charisma spoke softly to her mother. "Nothing would have been too big for Him to fix. I wish I would have told you," she said, gently stroking her mother's hair. She pulled Dafney's arm that was hanging over the edge of the bed and put it around her. She wept for her mother that she never got to know and will now never know.

When Charisma could find no more tears to cry, she just lay there and breathed in the familiar smell that she knew all too well. Her mother's favorite perfume...*Poison*.

CHAPTER FOURTEEN
SO CALLED FAMILY

The family was making their rounds and showing heartfelt sympathies and regret toward Charisma. However, in the background, she could hear low mumbles and whispers from her family with their personal opinions about the situation.

"Poor child, she had no clue," she heard one person say. "It doesn't make any sense. Why didn't they tell her? She had the right to know," someone else said. The worst comment was when someone said, "It's a good thing they never told her. I heard the mother was a drug addict. What kind of an example would that have been to the poor child?"

Charisma's eyes began to sting, and a tear rolled down her cheek. Not for the death of her mother, but for the misunderstanding that she left behind. She just sat in the front of the church staring at her mother's casket. Privately, she was wishing that her mother would somehow wake up and excitedly grab her by the arm saying, "Come on, let's go out. Let's go have some fun. Life waits for no woman you know." She smiled to herself as she remembered Dafney's favorite phrase.

Charisma was distraught and wished this funeral would soon be over. She was tired of people coming up to her and telling her how sorry they were for her, then going to the back of the funeral home gossiping about her mother with the rest of the family. Just as she finished that thought, here came someone else.

"It's going to be okay, Charisma!" One of her aunts came up to her practically yelling while rubbing her arm. Charisma figured that since she was in mourning, and not her normal outspoken and cheerful self, everyone must have thought she was deaf too. Everyone was talking to her as if there was a three-inch bulletproof glass between them.

"We understand your pain. Just remember everything happens for a reason," her aunt told her.

"*What does she mean she understands my pain?*" Charisma thought to herself. "*How can she possibly understand what I'm going through? Was she raised by parents that she now finds out really aren't her parents? Did her cool cousin really turn out to be her mother? No. I don't think so. So, how can she possibly know my pain?*" She angrily said to herself.

Everyone's personal thoughts and advice were just about to get on her last nerve. Finally, the Pastor took his place at the pulpit and the sermon began.

Lena and Devin sat on either side of Charisma trying to be her support system. Little did they know, the only person she would have rather been there was her boyfriend, Ivan, who she asked not to come. She wasn't ready to introduce him to her parents. Especially not during this type of occasion.

While the Pastor was giving his sermon, Charisma couldn't help but to wonder, *"How well do I really know this family? "They lied to me for 18 years. How can I ever trust them again?"*

"Charisma?... Charisma," her mother, Lena, whispered trying to get her attention. "It's time for you to give the eulogy.

She slowly made her way over to the pulpit and looked out amongst all the family. She also saw some of Dafney's model friends. She felt the urge to ask everyone for their forgiveness and tell them she could not go on with the eulogy.

Just then the door to the church swung open and in walked Franky. He gave her a wink, letting her know that it was alright, then took a seat in the back of the church.

Charisma took a deep breath and began. "As you all know by now, Dafney was my mother. I only knew her as such for a few hours. But as my cousin, I knew her a lifetime. From what I did get to see of her, I admired her a great deal. I thought she was beautiful and kind, and I could never understand it at the time, but in some ways, she seemed motherly toward me. I guess now I know why. I wrote a poem in her honor.

It's called:

From the Heart
I need the last piece to this puzzle.
The one that will make this picture complete.
Too long I have been wandering with no definite location.
My heart is so incomplete.

There is no question about it, this was not meant to be.
I now know that all this time,
I have been fighting against faith and destiny.
Two of which you can never win.
Now me, the loser in this game,
must accept defeat or forfeit,
and let what was meant to be, be.

With a tear in her eye, Charisma looked over at her mother lying there in the casket and immediately felt a surge of anger shoot up her spine. She decided to say some things that were really on her mind.

"I must be honest with you all. It is very difficult for me to stand here before my so-called family and give a eulogy for a woman that I found out was my mother, hours before she took her own life. I listened to many of you this evening bad talk my mother at her own funeral." Charisma's voice cracked and her tears began to flow.

Lena was getting up from her seat to relieve Charisma of the torture of being up there when Devin pulled her back down and whispered in her ear. "Leave her be. The child is right, and she needs to get this out. Let her do this, Lena, just let her do this."

Charisma waited for Lena to sit back down then continued. "Every one of you came up to me this evening telling me how sorry you are for me and how you understand my pain. What I don't understand is why people say things that they truly don't mean? If you all truly understood my pain like you say, then you would have all tried to avoid this pain that I'm feeling." Everyone stayed quiet, shocked at the severity in Charisma's voice.

"No one here understands what I'm going through. I wish you would all stop saying that you do and just leave me alone. Right now, I don't know what's real and what's not anymore. I don't know who's family and who's not. The only thing that I do know for sure is that the one person who was related to me, who was my mother, is now dead and I wish I was with her."

Then she walked over to the casket where her mother lay and spoke, "I miss you, mom. I miss you a whole lot. I wish you would have never done this, but I can imagine the pain of this world got the best of you. I just wish I could have gotten to know you better in a mother daughter kind of way. I guess life really doesn't wait for no woman, huh? Well, I love you. I loved you as my cousin and even more, I love you as my mother."

She leaned over the casket and kissed her mother on the cheek. Then she turned around and walked straight out of the church without ever turning to look back.

CHAPTER FIFTEEN
REALITY CHECK

"Do you need a ride?" She heard a voice say behind her. When Charisma turned around, she saw Franky's familiar face.

"Oh, thanks, but I think I can handle it, Franky."

"You know you are just as stubborn as she was. What makes you think you can sit here at the bus stop with let me see..." He paused and began to count the bags of groceries that Charisma had with her. "Six bags of groceries, get on the bus, and then walk them to the apartment," he continued.

"Well, I just have to do what I have to do, don't I?" She answered calmly.

"You and what army?"

"I don't need no army, Franky. I've been taking care of myself for the past four months. And I will continue to take care of myself, by myself, with no help from you or anybody else.

"Charisma, I'm gonna say this once. Give me your bags and get in the car and let me take you home," Franky said in a fatherly tone.

Charisma shook her head in disbelief. She laughed under her breath as she got up from the bench at the bus stop.

She walked over to where Franky stood, and with sureness in her voice, she said, "You know what, Franky, let me straighten you out a bit. That whole macho attitude might have been a little intimidating when we first met nine months ago. And it might have worked on my mother, but it won't work on me. You got that? I've been through a little too much shit to take anymore from you. I don't work for you and I'm not one of your hoes. So, I think you should just back off now while you have the chance." She grabbed her bags and began to walk to the next bus stop just to get away from him.

Franky rushed to catch up to her and said, "Look, Charisma that must have come out wrong..."

"You think?" She retorted, not even looking in his direction.

"Charisma, I'm just trying to help. That's the way that I am... but I guess the way I say things come off bitter sometimes."

Charisma wanted so badly to believe him, but she knew it was all a bunch of crap, so she continued on her way without a word.

"Please," he said, grabbing her by the arm. "Give me a chance, I'm not that bad."

"Yes, Franky, yes! You are *that* bad."

"Charisma, you're acting like this because of what happened with your cousin."

"My mother, Franky! She was my mother!" Charisma turned around and screamed at him with tears welling up in her eyes.

Franky could see the pain and hurt that she was carrying and truly felt sorry for her.

"Charisma, don't you think I'm hurting? I loved her too."

"No, you didn't, Franky. You never loved her. You only loved what you could get from her," she shouted.

"So, you think I was using her? If I were using her, do you think she would have all the things that she had? Look at the place where she lived. The place where you're living now. Anything you touch in that apartment, I bought.

Those words stung Charisma like a knife. Just to know that she was staying somewhere that truly wasn't hers, and at worst Franky's, made her cringe. But she had nowhere else to stay.

She pretty much broke things off with Ivan since the funeral. She has been trying to keep to herself and get her life together to start college next semester. She'd been working a part time job at a restaurant near the apartment so that she could save some money and pay what little bills she needed to pay.

"So, what are you saying, Franky? You want me out of the apartment?"

"Charisma," he laughed. "You really look at me like a monster, don't you? How could you possibly think that I would put the daughter of one of my good friends out on the street? I'm trying to tell you... that's not the way I am," he said, cracking a smile.

"So, what is it that you want then, Franky? I mean, what is all this about?"

"I just want you to be a little more appreciative, that's all. You just seem so ungrateful. I don't get a phone call, not even a thank you for all that I've done. Now, here you are arguing with me like I did something to hurt you."

Charisma was slightly confused. Since she came to New York she'd only seen Franky maybe five times total. The last time was at her mother's funeral. *So, what does he mean all he's done for me?* She thought to herself. She decided to just ask him. "Um, Franky, look I don't mean to be rude but what all have you done for me?"

Franky looked at her cunningly and asked, "For the past four months that you've been living in the apartment after Dafney died, have you paid rent?"

Charisma felt like she needed something to hold on to. She was so bewildered by the question. She was new at living on her own, never had to pay rent before, and it just slipped her mind. She didn't know if it was paid off already or what. No one had said anything to her, so she just bought groceries and essentials for the house, not thinking about anything else.

She felt really bad for the way she treated Franky, and he could tell. "Franky, I really apologize for my attitude. I had no clue. I've just been under a lot of stress lately."

"Don't you think I know this, Charisma? That's why I've been trying to take care of everything for you. To help relieve some of your stress; to help you out."

"And I thank you so much for it, Franky. Really, I do," she said, gratefully. "But you really don't have to do this anymore. I mean, I've got a job."

"Charisma, do you really think that job you have at the restaurant is going to pay the rent for that apartment plus all your necessities?"

At first, she wondered how he knew about her job at the restaurant. Then, she thought about what he said and was embarrassed. She knew that she wouldn't be able to pay the rent for that expensive apartment.

Seeing her embarrassment and knowing how prideful she was, Franky took the bags from her and led her to his car. Without a word, she followed.

When they arrived at the apartment, Franky helped Charisma take the groceries inside and put them away. He looked around the apartment and complimented her on how well kept it was. He told her, in all the times that he'd come to this apartment, it's never looked so neat.

Confused, Charisma told him how nice the place was when she first got there from Florida. Franky laughed before he answered.

"Your mother wasn't much of a homemaker, Charisma. I used to hire a housekeeper to come and clean this place once every two weeks and sometimes even that wasn't enough." She smiled as she remembered the times she'd cleaned up just to find the place in a mess all over again.

As they finished putting the groceries away, she actually enjoyed his company. She hadn't had anyone over besides the times Ivan came over trying to talk to her, wondering what he did wrong.

"Would you like a drink or something to eat?" She asked Franky. She was happy that she had someone there that she could talk to.

"Sure, but I don't think you have what I want."

"Try me," Charisma proudly answered.

"Okay, missy, do you have any beer?" Already knowing the answer, he laughed.

"No, but I do have a bottle of Moscato," she replied.

Surprised at Charisma's answer, Franky asked, "What are you doing with Moscato? I thought you didn't drink."

"I didn't," she answered, handing Franky a glass of wine, and sitting down to drink some of her own. "But with all that I've been going through lately I just kind of need something to...you know...kind of dull the pain a little bit."

"I understand... Oh wait, let me not say that. From the way you went off on your family at the funeral, I better not even try to understand."

"Shut up! Was I that bad?" Charisma questioned while getting comfortable on the sofa and tucking her feet underneath her.

"Please, you should have seen the look on everyone's face after you walked out of the church. I mean, no one said anything for a good two minutes."

"Honestly, Franky, I didn't mean to come off like that. I was just fed up."

"Why are you lying to me, Charisma? You know you meant every last word that came out of your mouth." They both laughed like two old friends.

"You know, I'm kind of glad we ran into each other today," Charisma admitted. "It's been rough being alone for these past couple of months."

"What happened with your family and your boyfriend?" He questioned.

"Well, with my boyfriend, I broke it off for now. I can't give him the attention that he really needs and deserves. I've got so much on my mind and it's a little hard for the boyfriend/girlfriend scene for me right now. You know what I mean?

As for my family, I haven't spoken to any of them since the funeral. I just want to be alone, and I guess find myself…who I am, and where I belong. You know?"

"I do, but your boyfriend - does he understand? Did you explain yourself to him or did you just drop him, leaving him wondering why?

Feeling guilty, Charisma changed the subject. "So, how's the modeling business coming along?"

"It's going well. I just wondered why you didn't pursue the invitation that I offered you."

"I don't know, Franky. I just don't think it's for me."

"Well, the invitation is open whenever you decide you want to make more than you're making at the restaurant." He drank down the rest of his drink and asked Charisma if she needed anything before he left.

"No, thank you. I'll be alright."

"What are you going to eat tonight?"

"I can grab something from the restaurant."

"How about I come pick you up later and cook dinner for you at my house?"

Feeling comfortable, Charisma agreed. "Thanks, I'd like that. What else do I have to do tonight? Nothing at all. Do you need me to bring anything?"

"No, just your appetite and pretty smile."

Charisma blushed at the comment. She was actually excited to be going somewhere for a change.

She walked him to the door, and he kissed her on the forehead and left.

CHAPTER SIXTEEN
POOR IVAN

After she cleaned up the house, Charisma was looking for something to wear to her dinner date with Franky when she heard the doorbell ring. She peeked through the peephole and quickly turned around with her hands over her chest. Holding her heart, she leaned her back against the door.

"Ivan, what are you doing here?" She asked nervously through the door.

"Charisma, I need to talk to you. Please, honey, let me in," he begged.

"Ivan, this isn't the time. I'm not ready to go back to how we were yet. I'm just not ready."

"But Charisma, that's just what I'm talking about. Things aren't going to be how they were. They will never be how they were. You've had a big change in your life, and everything is going to be new to you now. That's where I thought I came in. I thought I could be there for you during this new change in your life. You need me, honey. Let me be there for you. Please let me be the shoulder you cry on when you're lonely."

Charisma's heart went out to him. She knew he was telling the truth. She knew that he was what she needed but she still wanted to be alone. Charisma didn't want to bring Ivan into her mixed-up and confused world of lies and betrayal. But most of all, she was embarrassed. Embarrassed to face him again after all that she'd been through.

First, her cousin, who ended up really being her mother got high on ecstasy one night and had to be taken off by the ambulance. At the same time, her boyfriend lay dead from a drug overdose in the upstairs room of someone else's house that they didn't even know.

Then a couple months later, that same newfound mother commits suicide with sleeping pills. Leaving her daughter distraught and confused with no answers.

"This is like a damn soap opera. My whole life is like a flippin' soap opera," she thought to herself with her back still leaning against the door. *"How can I possibly face him like this?"*

"Ivan?" She questioned. "I don't know how. I don't know how to face you."

"You just open the door and let me take it from there, Charisma. Just open the door," he answered.

Charisma felt like she owed him an explanation anyway, so she opened the door, stepped aside, and let him in. "Alright, Ivan, we can talk, but not for long. I have plans."

Charisma figured if she told Ivan that she had plans he would realize that she wasn't making any promises to him, and they were just talking. Ivan felt a twinge of jealousy and wanted to ask what kind of plans. But he knew to take things one step at a time.

"Look Charisma, I'm not blaming you for wanting to spend some time apart. I can understand that you've been through a lot. But it's been nearly four months now and I haven't even received a phone call from you. I have no clue what's going on and I'm beginning to wonder if I did something to hurt you... Did I do something to hurt you?" He asked, walking over to Charisma who was still standing next to the front door. He took her hands in his.

"No, Ivan, of course not," she said, quickly taking her hand away from him.

"Then why haven't you returned any of my calls? Why the cold shoulder, Charisma? It must be me. Or something I did because this isn't making any sense. One minute, we're in love, having the greatest relationship of our lives. The next minute... nothing," he said with a lot of hurt in his voice.

"It's not you, Ivan. It's nothing to do with you treating me bad or anything like that. It's just that...I care for you so much...but right now, I can't be the girlfriend that you want me to be. I mean... you'll need my time, my attention, affection, and lots more and I can't give you my all right now."

"Charisma, I understand that. I don't expect you to give me your all right now. I want to be there for *you*. You need time to grieve, and I can give you as much time as you need. But please let me be there for you. Let me be the shoulder you cry on."

She felt herself about to break down and decided to cut the conversation short before that happened. She refused to cry in front of Ivan. That was one thing that Dafney taught her while she was posing as her cousin. *"Never let a man see you cry,"* she remembered her mother saying. *"Because once you allow him to see you cry, you've shown him your weakest part of your being. Which means, you've given him the key to your heart, bringing him too close to you and your personal life. You never give a man the key to your heart, nor do you let a man get that close to knowing you or your personal life, no matter how much you love him."*

"Look, Ivan, I think that's it for tonight. I'll call you later and we can talk some more," she suggested.

Hurt… Ivan just looked at her, walked over to the front door, and stepped out into the hallway. He turned around and said, "I'm not giving up on you that easy, Charisma. I do love you and I'm a very hard man to get rid of when I'm in love."

CHAPTER SEVENTEEN
A NIGHT TO REMEMBER

Stepping into Franky's house was like stepping into another dimension. He had many rooms, each with a different personality.

One room, which Charisma took as her favorite, was the African room as Franky called it. It had beautiful pieces of African art on the walls of strong black women. One in particular really caught her eye. It was a woman with a baby wrapped in a white cloth and tied across her chest. She squatted in the river and washed her clothes with a beautiful look of contentment on her face.

She gazed at the woman in the picture and wished she could ask her what was there to be so happy about? She's obviously struggling to make ends meet, washing clothes in a river with a baby tied to her body, and yet she looks happy.

Charisma just could not understand how someone could smile at a time when things seemed so low. Deep in her thoughts, she felt the eyes of someone watching her. She turned around to Franky, leaning against the doorway.

"She's my favorite too. Don't you love the way she seems to have everything under control? She's my kind of a woman."

Charisma nodded her head in agreement, not sure of what Franky meant by his comment.

"So, are you ready for a scrumptious meal that you will never forget?"

Charisma was very hungry and looking forward to the meal. But the way that Franky said that, sent a slight chill up her spine. She didn't let it bother her though because she had learned to trust him.

"Come on into the kitchen. Let me show you what I threw together," Franky told her, taking her by the arm.

"What you threw together? Are you sure you can cook? I would like to walk out of here the same way that I walked in... healthy," Charisma said jokingly.

"Oh, trust me you'll walk out of here better than when you walked in," he answered with a smile.

That same chill returned. Charisma swore she could hear a faint voice in her head pleading with her to leave. She had become so used to Franky, his mood swings and off the wall comments, that she figured she knew how to deal with them. She blew his comment off and followed him into the kitchen.

"Mmm, it smells fabulous in here. What did you cook?" Charisma asked, surprised that Franky really had cooking skills.

"Well, I tried to make a special dinner for a very special friend. I made curry coconut shrimp with white rice and a vegetable medley," Franky announced proudly, opening up the pot with the shrimp to show off his cooking skills. "I even poured the gravy on the side just in case the curry was too strong for your liking. Then, for dessert, I made Flan."

"Flan? Now I know you didn't do all this by yourself!" Charisma said, letting out a squeal of laughter.

Showing true to his mood swings, Franky exploded. "I go through this whole ordeal of cooking a special dinner for you and all you've done since you've been here is criticize and complain. I'm quite sick of it!" Then he stormed out of the kitchen and into the dining room.

Charisma's mouth flew open speechless. She was keenly aware of Franky's temper and didn't know what came over her acting the way she did. She knew the best thing, at the moment, was an apology. She pushed through the swinging doors of the kitchen and sat down on the couch next to him.

"Look, Franky, I didn't mean to upset you. I was only joking around. I mean, I really appreciate all that you've done for me… the rent, this dinner, everything. You have truly been there for me, and I guess I felt a little uncomfortable because there's no way for me to repay you."

"Charisma, I never asked you to repay me. I was a friend of your mother's and now that she's gone, I choose to continue my friendship to her by helping you, her daughter."

"Thanks, Franky. I really am grateful to you for everything. You're not what I expected from the first day I met you. I thought you were kind of a real jerk, but you've proven me wrong. You really do have a heart."

"And you've proven me wrong as well."

"I have? In what way?"

"Well, when I first met you, I thought you were a spoiled girl from the country who knew nothing about what real life was all about. But, to my surprise, you've truly grown up these past couple of months. You seem so much more mature and aware of your surroundings."

"Thanks, Franky. Thats a great compliment coming from you," Charisma said, beaming from his comment.

Franky leaned in closer to Charisma on the couch and put his arm around her in a loving embrace. Then he brushed his hand over Charisma's breast. She tensed up very quickly and wasn't sure whether it was an accident or if he had done it on purpose. At least until Franky pulled Charisma's face towards his to kiss her. Charisma jerked away and immediately stood up.

"What are you doing?!" She screamed, with her heart pounding.

"What's the problem? You've kissed me before," Franky asked.

"Yes, but I was stupid then. I made a mistake.

"Okay, you're right," he announced with his hands up in the air. Let's just continue our date and eat like we planned and enjoy the evening. Okay?"

"Date? Franky, I wouldn't call this a date. I'd call it a dinner between two friends..."

Before Charisma could blink, Franky dashed at her and grabbed her by the arm.

"What do you mean a dinner between two friends?" He scowled at her. "If I want to say that we're on a date, then we're on a date. What? Do you think that you're too good to date me?" He asked Charisma as she looked on in complete terror. "Answer me!" He snapped. Do you feel that your ungrateful ass is too good for me?"

"N-No, Franky, I was just straightening out the situation," Charisma answered. Now she was wishing she had listened to that little voice in her head earlier telling her to leave.

"Just straightening out the situation?" He mocked her. "Well let me straighten you out, CHA-RIS-MA. Neither you nor your dead mother were too good for me, okay? So, I'd advise that you bring that nose of yours down out of the clouds. Without me, your mother wouldn't have made it as far as she did."

When Franky mentioned her mother in the horrible tone that he used, Charisma's fear of him was instantaneously replaced with anger. She answered him in a steady voice.

"You brag that without you my mother wouldn't have made it as far as she did. But the truth of the matter, FRAN-KY, is that without you my mother wouldn't be where she is right now and that's dead!" She grabbed her purse, and finally listened to that voice in her head and headed for the door.

"Charisma, I wouldn't go out that door if I were you."

"Well, you're not me, Franky."

"But if I were you, I would be smart enough to know a good thing when I have one. I would be smart enough to turn around when the man who's paying my rent and all my bills says turn around."

Charisma stopped, clenching her teeth as she thought about what he said. She slowly turned to face him as she gave up her fight and submissively gave in to Franky's wishes.

Feeling proud that he had won this round and gotten his way, he became kind again. Pointing her in the direction of the bathroom, he said, "why don't you head to the restroom and wash up while I get the food on the table?"

As Charisma headed down the hall, she wondered how she had ever got herself into this situation. *"What am I doing here? I knew this man was crazy. How could I have been so stupid to come here to his house, much less alone. Charisma, you are so stupid!"* She silently scolded herself.

"What? Did you feel like you owed him your presence because he's been paying your rent for the past four months? For this,

you could have stayed with Ivan, instead of now worrying about your safety," continuing with the self-ridicule.

When Franky saw that Charisma was finally out of sight, he quickly got to work. He beautifully dressed both plates and placed them on the table. Then, he quickly poured two glasses of champagne. But in Charisma's glass, he dropped a small white pill that easily dissolved in with all the bubbles. Then he continued to set the mood for the evening.

Meanwhile, in the bathroom, Charisma looked frantically for something to protect herself if push came to shove. She searched through all of Franky's cabinets and found nothing. He was so meticulous; nothing was out of place.

She became desperate and quickly rummaged through the waste basket. She found a little silver razor blade, still in the black razor. *"Perfect!"* She said to herself. She tried breaking the plastic to get the blade out, but it was a disposable razor and was not easy.

Working very quickly, before Franky began to wonder what happened to her, she snapped the head of the razor, finally freeing the blade from its place. Charisma was so elated to have finally gotten it free that she hadn't noticed the blood running down her wrist. When she became aware, she was frightened to see that her wound was so deep that her blood was dripping on Franky's white Angora bath rug.

She hastily ran her hand under cold water and searched through the cabinets again. This time for a first aid kit. She knew that she had already been in there over ten minutes and Franky would come looking for her soon. She hurried to dress her wounds and clean up the mess that she had made on the rug. As soon as that thought passed through her head, she heard his voice. "Charisma, are you alright in there? Dinner is getting cold."

With her heart beating fast, she quickly turned the rug around where the stained part would be hidden by the overlay of Franky's cabinets under the sink. Then, she hurriedly put the band-aid that she found in his medicine cabinet around her thumb hoping that it was enough to stop the bleeding.

"Charisma!" Franky shouted at the door, beginning to get irritated since he received no answer.

Right then, Charisma opened the door with a perfect smile on her face. In an almost flirty manner, to take Franky's mind off her lengthy bathroom visit, she said, "Geesh Franky, can't a girl have some privacy around here." Pulling the door closed behind her, she was standing right before his face. She was hoping to distract him from going into the bathroom and seeing the mess she had left behind.

Charisma's plan worked all too well because Franky forgot about everything, including his irritation. He stepped in closer to her and looked deep into her eyes. "You seem to have had a change of heart."

Feeling very disgusted, Charisma had no choice but to smile and play along. She knew Franky's other side. Dr. Jeckell could show up at any time so gazing back into his eyes, she quickly but calmly answered him. "I guess I did, didn't I? I mean, how often do you get to have a handsome and successful man cook and serve you dinner these days?"

With a huge grin on his face, Franky took her hand, pulled her close to him, and passionately kissed her. While Charisma would rather be gutting dead fish with her bare hands, she sucked it up and kissed him back as if he was the man she had been waiting for all her life. She knew that her main goal was to get safely out of his home and to never ever have to see him again.

Feeling like a million bucks after their kiss, Franky led Charisma by the hand into the dining room. She found a beautifully set table with lit candles and food displayed so wonderfully she almost didn't want to eat it. She was so impressed that she began to think that maybe this night might not be so bad after all.

Franky pulled out her chair and very gentlemanly laid her napkin on her lap. He went to his seat and did the same for himself.

Charisma felt very special at this point. She felt that the blade she still held between her thumb and her forefinger was no longer necessary. She discreetly put it away in her pocket.

Raising his glass toward Charisma, Franky announced, "let's toast to a beautiful night with a beautiful woman."

As they clinked glasses and Charisma was taking a sip, she noticed Franky watching her very strangely. As she placed her glass back on the table and was ready to take a bite of her salad, she immediately felt a warm rush come over her.

Charisma assumed she sipped her champagne too quickly, especially on an empty stomach. But then a tingling sensation took over her whole body and her hands began to feel numb.

She chose not to say anything to Franky about how she was feeling. She had already been through an embarrassing situation with him and her inability to handle her alcohol. She had made a complete fool of herself and refused to let it happen again. So, with determination, she picked up her salad fork and dove right into eating her salad.

Charisma was ready to compliment Franky on the beautiful evening and how great the salad was even though she couldn't seem to taste a thing. But when she looked up, she couldn't focus on him. It was as if her eyes were moving too fast for her brain to focus on the figure that sat before her.

When she opened her mouth to call Franky's name, she heard her own voice echoing loudly in her head. She knew something wasn't right.

"Franky, something is wrong with me," she could hear herself say.

"No, Charisma, nothing is wrong with you. Nothing is wrong at all. I usually keep my promises, don't I?"

"Franky, what are you talking about?" Charisma asked, confused. She started to feel the numbness in her arms move throughout her entire body.

"Well, I said earlier you would be leaving here better than when you walked in."

A rush of terror ran through her veins. Now, she completely understood what Franky meant by his earlier comments. Frightened, she tried to stand up and run to safety. She got to the door, reached for the handle, and noticed something strange happening.

The door seemed to be moving further and further away from her. Her body almost felt like it was floating high into the air. All of a sudden, Charisma's head felt really heavy. She realized she was hanging upside down. She forced her eyes open to find herself facing the back of Franky's denim shirt and understood what was happening.

He was carrying her over his shoulder. Carrying her away…away from safety. If she could just reach the doorknob and turn it. It would take her back… back to life outside this apartment and what was about to happen to her.

CHAPTER EIGHTEEN
FRANKY'S BED

The morning sun shone brightly through the windows as Charisma wiped her eyes. Her head felt heavy, and her eyes were still finding it hard to focus on her surroundings. If she stared at something long enough, she noticed that the object began to come into sight.

She sat up slowly and looked around the room to find she was in Franky's bedroom. Trying to replay the scene of last night in her head, she willed herself to remember exactly what happened that would put her in this room... in Franky's bedroom.

Looking around for evidence, Charisma could not find that the sheets were disheveled in any awkward kind of way. The room was perfect, as perfect as the rest of Franky's house. Then, why was she here?

Charisma's head started to spin again. She lay back down on the soft down comforter to ease the nauseousness she was beginning to feel.

"Think, Charisma, think. What happened? Did you drink too much? What happened to you last night? Why are you still here?"

When her head started to feel better, she slowly got up to find Franky and get some answers to her questions. As she opens the door, the wonderful smell of bacon was coming from the kitchen. She held on to the wall, walking toward the direction of the smell.

"Good morning, sunshine!" Franky nearly shouted at her.

"Franky, can you tell me why I'm still here?"

"What do you mean why are you still here? You spent the night, remember?"

"No, actually I don't," she said, rubbing her eyes. She was looking around his house almost searching for something, anything that would help trigger her memory.

Franky noticed her searching eyes and trying to distract her, offered her some breakfast. She accepted and sat down to eat. She cringed from the pain she felt radiating from her private section.

She excused herself and headed to the bathroom down the hall that she used last night. While relieving herself, she looked around the bathroom and saw the mess she left there last night and her memory was triggered. She remembered looking for something… something to protect herself in case Franky tried to harm her. But did he? Did he harm her? She couldn't remember anything about last night and began to worry.

As she stood to flush the toilet, she noticed blood in the toilet. She squinted and tried hard to focus her eyes on what she was seeing. She could not understand why she would be bleeding. Her period was not due for another three weeks or so.

Charisma began to feel sick. She knew she needed to get home. She headed back to the kitchen to tell Franky that she was leaving. As she walked out of the bathroom, Franky was standing right there in front of the door.

"Oh, Franky! You startled me. Why are you standing here like this?"

"Are you feeling, okay?" He asked her in a serious, almost uncaring tone.

"Yeah, a little better, but I'm still curious about what happened last night."

"I told you that you spent the night."

"See, that's just the thing, Franky. I don't remember having any intentions of spending the night here. I don't see why I would not just go home."

Thinking quickly, Franky said, "Charisma, you know you can't handle your liquor. So, you just stayed the night here rather than go home in your condition.

"In my condition, huh?" She questioned, starting to realize Franky wasn't being completely honest with her. "I really don't remember drinking that much last night," she stated. She was starting to feel a little better and more like herself again. "I thought all we had last night was champagne and dinner. What else am I missing, Franky?" Charisma questioned, angrily.

Simone K. Baker

"Why am I sore all over my body, Franky? Why do I feel like I've been hit by a truck? And more importantly, why am I bleeding?" She questioned him, her voice getting louder. She found herself walking up on him.

"Charisma, I'm telling you what happened so you can calm down. You ate dinner with me, we sat down on the couch to talk and had a drink. When you said you had a headache, I helped you into my bed and let you sleep. I came out to the couch and stayed there all night."

Charisma walked toward the living room and found her purse on the side of the couch. She grabbed it and headed for the door. As she pulled the door open, she heard Franky call her name.

She stopped and gave him the chance to say what he needed to say before she left.

"Charisma, I wouldn't say anything about what happened last night to anybody if you know what's good for you."

Her hand froze on the doorknob. She felt her legs wanting to go out from under her. She closed her eyes and told herself to get it together and walk out of there. To walk out and never ever return!

CHAPTER NINETEEN
A TRUE FRIEND

"Charisma, I don't care what you say, we need to get you to the emergency room and have you checked out. For all we know, this man could have slipped you something and raped you and you would know none the less."

Charisma's mind ran wild. She had called Ivan as soon as the taxi dropped her home and told him everything that happened or what she could remember. Ivan told her to stay where she was, he would be there in ten minutes. True to his word, Ivan was knocking on the door before she could blink.

When Charisma let him in, she could remember how he just pulled her into his arms and hugged her right there in the doorway. No words, nothing. Just silence and a much-needed hug. She knew she could trust him and was so grateful that he never gave up on her.

Ivan stepped away from Charisma to get a good look at her. She felt so naked. She was embarrassed to face him. Until now, she was a virgin and wasn't sure if she still was anymore. She knew he was thinking the same thing.

"Charisma, it's okay," he said, lovingly looking at her. "If what we think happened, we can get through this. Okay? I'm here for you. I'm not going anywhere, I promise." For the first time, despite what Dafney tried to teach her, Charisma buried her face in Ivan's chest and cried her eyes out.

She cried for her mother. She cried for wanting to go to school. She cried for her parents. She cried for her future. But most importantly, she cried for herself. For this innocent girl from the country who was told not to come to this city but never listened. Now, she's suffering…. suffering the consequences. She truly had no chance.

"Charisma… Charisma," Ivan called. "Do you understand what I'm saying, honey? We need to get you to the emergency room. There are so many things we need to get checked. They will be able to tell you if something happened. I'll be right there but we have to go before all the evidence is gone from your body, if there is any."

Walking with Ivan the short distance downstairs to his car was a little painful. She didn't feel the pain as badly before because she was so confused and dysfunctional. As time went by, and she was home in her own element, Charisma noticed all the different sore spots of her body.

Inwardly, Charisma didn't need a doctor to tell her what she already knew. That Franky had done something to her. It became even more apparent to her by the raw way her private parts felt but she refused to say anything to Ivan. He had already been through so much with her. She thought it was better for him, the longer she could keep this reality from him.

"Next!" The woman behind the glass called out to Charisma and Ivan who were standing behind the red line. Scared and unsure, Charisma looked over at Ivan for reassurance as he nodded for her to go ahead. "I'm right here," he whispered.

"Yes ma'am, my name is Charisma Hennings. I would like to see a doctor please." Charisma barely whispered to the woman through the glass.

The woman noticed that something was terribly wrong with the young girl. In a calmer tone, she said, "okay honey, I just need to know what your trouble is. Are you sick?" she asked.

"No... I mean, yes...I mean, I don't think so."

"Well, why are you needing a doctor, sweetie?"

"I think I might have been raped?" Her voice quivered.

"You think?" The woman behind the glass nearly shouted with shock in her voice.

"Well, you see, I can't remember anything about last night and my body hurts all over."

She understood this kind of thing all too well. Being a nurse for as long as she has, the woman behind the glass had seen far too many of these date rape cases. Her heart went out to Charisma. "I'll take you down to room two. Is he with you?" She asked, pointing to Ivan.

"Yes ma'am, he is," Charisma said feeling uplifted knowing that Ivan was still there waiting with her.

CHAPTER TWENTY
I HAVE NOTHING

"Alright Charisma, your tests results are in," the doctor announced, walking into the examination room where they were left waiting.

Charisma squeezed Ivan's hand as her heart began to pound.

"It's okay, Charisma," Ivan whispered in her ear, smoothing down the back of her hair. He could sense her worry.

"The drug tests do show the remains of what we believe to be under the street name - ecstasy."

Charisma buried her face in Ivan's chest and began to cry. He hugged her tight while rubbing her back. He asked the doctor, "Does that mean...?"

"Yes, it does," the doctor interrupted. "We saw signs of intercourse when we were doing our examination, but we wanted to be sure and wait for the results," the doctor admitted.

Charisma cried harder hearing this devastating confirmation. In her heart, she already knew what had happened to her. Hearing it confirmed, just turned her stomach.

Charisma felt like her life was over. She had held on to her virginity waiting for her husband or the right man all her life. Now, it was gone forever. Taken by someone she never intended to give it to. By someone who never even asked. Someone who tricked her.

She felt violated and bitter. She just wanted to go home and sit under the shower and wash off any remnants of Franky that may be lingering on her body.

The doctor waited while Charisma composed herself then continued. "The good news is that it seems as though this person used protection because we found no signs of semen within the vaginal walls whatsoever. But that doesn't mean that we are completely clear of STD's. We need to wait for some more results to come back from the lab. But as of now, I'm feeling better about this case than I was."

Charisma just sat quietly listening to the doctor. Wishing that this was all a bad dream, and she would wake up any minute now.

"In another week, I would like you to come back in for some more tests. For now, the rest of the test results that we are waiting for should be in by tomorrow. We will give you a call if we notice anything abnormal," the doctor continued.

"What other test results are we waiting on?" Ivan questioned, still holding Charisma's face to his chest.

"For rape cases, there are a series of tests that we need to do by law. Some we get the answers to right away, others we have to wait a few days. But I'll tell you this, young lady, not all of these cases end as well as yours did. We have young women come through this hospital beat up pretty bad and, in some cases, dead."

Charisma was listening, but she was numb. She had already stopped herself from crying and was now listening to the doctor and Ivan go back and forth about her condition. She really didn't care what tests they had to do anymore. She already felt tainted and no longer like her old self anymore.

She heard the doctor mention that some cases don't end as *well* as hers did. That some end up dead. *But what was the difference between those girls and what she was feeling inside right now*, she thought to herself. She no longer had a gift to give. She was now just a girl. A tainted girl that had nothing to offer anyone... not even Ivan.

She wanted to take his hands off her. She wanted to scream at him and ask him - why was he still here? Why didn't he run? Especially now that he knew the truth.

"I'm a rape victim. Did he not hear the doctor just say that? Here is his chance to run, yet he's still standing here," she thought to herself.

"I'd like to leave now," they heard Charisma finally say from under Ivan's embrace.

"Yes, we will go ahead and get you discharged. But, Charisma, I need to ask you, do you want to go ahead and press charges?"

"...No" Charisma answered with no emotion in her voice.

"But Charisma, how could..."

"I said no, Ivan! Now please get me out of here and take me home," Charisma chimed in before Ivan could even get his words out.

"It's normal for you to feel this way, Charisma," the doctor interrupted. "I've worked many cases like yours and at first, the girls choose not to press charges. But after time, get the courage and decide the right thing to do. You need to think about the other girls that he's done this to. Most likely, if he did this to you, you're not the first. There are others and there will continue to be more after you. Why not be a part of stopping this man before he harms another young girl?"

"I'll think about it."

"That's all we can ask for. It's better than just no," the doctor said with a slight smile on his face. "Now, go straight home and get some rest. Please call us if you feel anything different or if you have any questions," the doctor said, patting Charisma on her arm before he left the room.

On the way home, Charisma was silent. So silent that it concerned Ivan. He noticed as soon as it was confirmed that Franky did take advantage of her, she became very distant. Even while hugging her in the hospital, he felt her whole body stiffen. He got the impression she wanted him to move away from her.

"Would you like me to stay the night with you?" Ivan asked as they entered the apartment.

"No, I'm okay, Ivan. Thanks. Thanks for coming with me to the hospital and for everything, really. I just want to go lie down and try to forget about this whole thing."

"Well, if that's what you really want," Ivan uttered. He was feeling crushed by Charisma's obvious attempt to get rid of him.

"Yes, that's what I want right now."

"What if I came by in the morning on my way to work and dropped off some breakfast?"

"I don't need breakfast, Ivan!" She snapped, before realizing the tone of her voice. Then she gently repeated, "I mean, I don't need breakfast. I just need some time. Some time away...alone. Time to heal."

"Look, Charisma I understand..."

"Do you understand, Ivan!?" She snapped again. Intentionally, this time. "Do you really understand? Here I am in this crazy city, barely a year, and I feel that I've lived more than I've lived in 18 years and not in a good way! Ivan, I lost my mother...I was raped...what do I have left? What more can I handle?"

He grabbed Charisma in his arms and held her tightly as she wept. He thought about her words and truly could not understand how she was feeling. He'd never experienced anything like what she was going through.

"Ivan, I need you to leave please," Charisma whispered from under his embrace.

"What?" Ivan stepped back to look at her and make sure he was hearing correctly.

"I want you to leave, and please, will you do something else for me?"

"What's that?" He asked.

"Never come back."

Ivan's heart felt like it was in his throat. He didn't know what to make of this. He understood that she had gone through many tragedies and had asked for space before. But this wasn't asking for space. This was asking him to leave her life for good.

"Charisma, do you know what you're saying?" Ivan pleaded.

"I know what I'm doing, Ivan. I have nothing…nothing else to give you, not anybody. I'm no longer a virgin, Ivan. I have no gift I can give you. I'm done."

"Charisma, please, we can work through this. I'm okay with you just the way you are."

"Ivan, get out my face and leave me alone!!! I have nothing else to give!" Charisma yelled at the top of her lungs.

Ivan was so shocked that he headed toward the door without another word. He desperately wanted to turn around and fight for her. But he knew at this point, there was no hope for that.

She really needed to be left alone with her thoughts. He stepped out of Charisma's apartment and into the hallway.

As he pulled the door behind him, he prayed to himself, *"If she's truly meant to be mine God, You will bring her back to me in Your time. Until then, I will patiently wait for you, Charisma. I will patiently wait...."*

CHAPTER TWENTY- ONE
THE SCARLETT LETTER

"Let me have your ID please," the man behind the cherry wood desk told Charisma.

"Yes, here it is. I turned 18, September 29th."

"You do know if I hire you, there will be no drinking."

"Yes, sir. I understand that completely."

"I'm not playing either. I'm not trying to lose my liquor license over some little fresh out of the water 18-year-old, who can't follow rules.

"You definitely don't have to worry about me. I follow rules very well," Charisma stated, trying very hard to impress the club manager.

Ever since she came back from the hospital finding out she was raped by Franky; she wanted no parts of him at all. Nothing to do with him whatsoever. But it was kind of hard when she knew she was living in an apartment that he was paying all the bills for.

Realizing this, she immediately became furious. She had searched the yellow pages all night, calling any and every business. She was looking for a job that would pay the rent and the utilities for this apartment. But she needed money for herself too, and nothing was offering to pay her enough to take care of her bills and herself. That is, until she came across an ad in the paper that said: *Make $2,000 a week and make your own schedule. Just call and ask for Jake.*

She had seen this place many times getting out of her taxi to go to work at the restaurant. She also knew many of the girls that worked there.

Many times, they would come into the restaurant to eat. They would always try to talk her into coming to work with them. They would flaunt their money and cars in front of her, but Charisma was never interested. It never crossed her mind because she was never in need of money.

Franky paid for everything and what he didn't pay, the money she made at the restaurant paid the rest. She was very content, but not anymore. Now, she refused to let him continue to pay the rent for that apartment.

She didn't want to move because she loved the memory the apartment gave her of her mother. But in order to stay in that expensive apartment and live the life she'd been living; she knew she would have to do something. Something very drastic. That's what gave her the final push to walk through the doors of the Scarlett Letter.

CHAPTER TWENTY-TWO
AND SO IT BEGINS

On Charisma's very first day at the Scarlett Letter, she walked through the front doors with her head held high. She was very nervous and afraid on the inside. She didn't know what to expect but refused to show any signs of fear in this place. She knew that as hard of a life as she'd been having, it could get even worse if she didn't handle herself accordingly in a place like this.

"Hello, how are you doing this evening? Welcome to the Scarlett Letter," she heard a very happy and kind voice say to her. She was shocked to see a very young-looking girl with blond, almost white hair and intense blue eyes smiling in her direction.

"Uh, hi... my name is Charisma and today... uh I mean, tonight is my first night."

"Oh yes, Jake told me you would be starting," the young girl said with a huge smile on her face. "Give me a moment to call Jake and have him come get you."

"Jake? Jake?" The girl called into her walkie talkie. "Charisma is here and ready to get started," she said, giving Charisma a wink.

While Charisma waited, she watched as men walked by her and were greeted by the overly excited young girl at the front. She watched them, watch her, as they paid the girl and walked through the heavy fancy glass doors. Every time that glass door opened, her nerves went crazy. She could hear laughter and the loud boom of the music. But it was so dark that she couldn't see anything but the glow of black lights.

"Charisma!" A man from behind startled her. She turned around and saw Jake in a suit and tie coming toward her with his arms wide open.

"Hey, honey you made it," Jake said, hugging her and completely confusing Charisma. "Let's go inside so I can show you around." Jake shows Charisma a huge smile, opens the heavy glass door and like a gentleman, lets her go in first.

Once she was inside those doors, Charisma looked around in amazement at all the activity going on. To her right was a table with a pole dead smack in the middle. On it was a woman swinging round and round with no fear, her brunette-colored hair catching up to each spin. There were men sitting around the table watching her and talking to one another in deep conversation.

Throughout the club, there were many tables like this. All with women in itty bitty bikinis spinning about as men watched. But the catcher was the main stage with huge, bright lights and a beautiful woman seductively dancing across the stage - NAKED.

Charisma stared at this woman in shock. She couldn't move anymore. It was like her feet were cemented to the ground. She heard Jake whisper in her ear, "Charisma, act cool. I know this is new to you. But, honey, don't stare and act like this. The men are watching."

Charisma looked around her and noticed she was definitely a minority in this room. Not because she was black, but because she was a woman in a room full of men. Yes, there were more women in this room, but she was the only one with her clothes still on.

Her heart began pounding immediately! Reality hit her! This is what she came here to do! She began to hyperventilate right there in the middle of the Scarlett Letter with all the men watching.

Jake looked around in a panic. He had never had this happen to him before. Girls came and went all the time. They looked around and either wanted to start or decided against it and just left. But never a scene like this in front of his clientele.

"Charisma? Charisma, is that you?" A half-naked girl came running up to her and Jake, covering her chest. "Jake, it's okay, I know her. I'll take care of her."

"Well, get her away from the men and do something," he retorted. "This is ridiculous."

"She'll be okay Jake. I'll take her in the back. Come on, Charisma. Come with me, honey." She gently led Charisma down a dark hallway away from the main room where all the music and men were. She led her into a less chaotic dressing room with women running around naked and paying no attention to young Charisma. She stood in the doorway staring with astonishment.

"Charisma, after all this time, I can't believe you actually came. This is so awesome."

Charisma's breathing finally slowed enough for her to focus. She realized the smiling face in front of her was Cherry from the restaurant. She was one of the girls that always came in trying to get her to come work with them.

"Cherry? Oh, my goodness is that you?" Charisma grabbed Cherry into a tight embrace.

"Charisma, it's going to be okay... calm down. I'm here now, I'll help you. Your main concern now is getting back on Jake's good side. You really embarrassed him out there."

"Oh, my goodness, I didn't mean to. This is all so... so.... different for me," she said, looking around the dressing room.

"Well, what did you expect when you came to work in a strip club, Mama?" Cherry laughed and tried to make light of the situation.

Hearing those words put a hard knot in Charisma's stomach. It was as if what she planned on doing wasn't real to her until someone actually placed her in the situation. All of a sudden, she was confused and unsure of herself.

"I guess you're right," Charisma said, feeling really embarrassed.

"No worries, honey, I'm just teasing you. We all went through this same thing. Just maybe not out on the floor...in front of the guest," she added with a chuckle.

Charisma was so happy to see Cherry that she was able to really take in what was going on around her. She noticed the women in the room were all acting normal and not anything like what she imagined or had seen on TV.

Some looked like moms with their reading glasses on in their chairs with their feet up. Reading as if they were at home very comfortably curled up with a good book. As if they didn't notice that beyond those doors there were men waiting to look at their bodies.

She was shocked to see pictures of their kids up on the mirrors. One woman was just coming in wearing jeans and a T-shirt. She was on the phone talking to what seemed to be her daughter. "Okay, honey, now make sure you brush your teeth and say your prayers. Then go straight to bed, okay? Alright, honey, mommy loves you so much, okay? Now put daddy on the phone please."

Daddy? Charisma thought to herself. *"There is a daddy? What man allows his wife to do this?"* Charisma questioned in her mind. Hearing that mother talk to her daughter on the phone while walking into a place like this shocked Charisma the most.

She never imagined that these women had normal lives. That some of them may have kids and families. How could someone that did this be and look so normal?

Simone K. Baker

Charisma looked up and saw her reflection in the mirror, but she didn't recognize herself. She was falling apart. This was low for her being in this place. *"Can I really go through with this?"* She asked herself. *"Do I even really want to?"*

"Sunflower!" She heard Cherry shout with excitement.

"What are you talking about, Cherry?" Charisma asked, a little shaken up from being snapped out of her daze.

"Sunflower! That's what you should call yourself!" Cherry shrieked with full excitement. You would have thought she had just guessed the correct answer on wheel of fortune to win the grand prize.

Charisma just looked at Cherry. She could see the happiness in her face. She was basically jumping up and down in front of her and Charisma really didn't want to disappoint her.

"Sunflower, huh? Wow, that sounds great." Charisma tried to be enthused but deep down, she felt like garbage. She thought to herself, *"What am I becoming? Where will this take me?"*

She took a deep breath and remembered her real focus for doing this was to get Franky off her back. She remembered what he did to her and that she wanted so badly to keep the apartment for her mother's memory. But she wanted to pay for it on her own with no help from Franky. If she never heard his name again, it would be too soon.

"Yeah, Sunflower is perfect. I like it."

"You do? Really, Charisma? That's great. I just knew it would fit you!" Cherry said, bursting with excitement and energy. "Listen, Charisma, give me your address. I'll come by tomorrow and pick you up. We'll go get some costumes for you and don't worry about the money. Just pay me back when you start making that money girl," Cherry told her, playfully pushing her in the shoulder.

"Thanks, Cherry. That is really thoughtful of you."

"Don't mention it. Any excuse to get out and go shopping is a great day for me," Cherry said, almost jumping up and down.

Charisma giggled as she watched Cherry acting like an animated character. She thought to herself, *"if anyone should be named Sunflower between the two of us, it should definitely be her."*

CHAPTER TWENTY-THREE
A BAD DREAM

"Hey, girlie! You're early," Charisma told Cherry when she opened the door.

"You'll learn that in our business we need to make the most of our days," Cherry responded, dancing through the door. "We need to get as much accomplished as possible because we work from the evening to all night most days."

"Wow, our business," Charisma thought to herself. *"So that wasn't a bad dream after all?"*

"This apartment is really nice," Cherry said snapping Charisma out of her thoughts. "But I can tell you right now, you are not affording this place by working in the restaurant, are you?" Cherry said, looking around intently at the apartment.

"No. I'm not," Charisma admitted sadly.

"No need to be sad, honey. The Scarlett Letter is about to hook you up!" They both laughed.

"Give me a moment, Cherry. Just let me run and grab my purse real quick."

She ran to the bedroom to grab her purse but made a beeline for the bathroom. Before she knew it, she was bent over the toilet. She was vomiting everything she ate that morning which wasn't very much because she hadn't been feeling very well.

She quickly cleaned herself up, grabbed her purse, and headed out the door with Cherry.

"Girl, you feeling okay?" Cherry asked Charisma once they headed into the first store at the mall.

"Yeah, just feeling a little dizzy. I might need to grab a bite to eat in a bit."

"Sure, no problem. Let's just get a couple of things here, then we'll head out to the food court."

"Sounds like a plan," Charisma said with a smile. She was so happy to finally have a friend in this big city.

She knew she had a great friend in Ivan, but she had to let him go. He was too normal and too great of a guy for her upside-down life. She began to feel guilty remembering the morning at the hospital. Ivan waited by her side for hours while they tested, probed, and checked her, only to find out she was raped by Franky.

Although Charisma was happy that he was there for her, it was embarrassing for her to even look Ivan in the face afterward. She felt humiliated and less than a woman. Charisma prided herself on her virginity and held it dearly to her heart and now it was gone. She was beginning to love Ivan. She dreamed of the day she would give him this special gift she had for him, but not anymore.

What could he possibly want from her now? She felt disgusting. After he dropped her off at the apartment, she could tell he wanted to stay but she pushed him away and out of her life for the second and final time.

Charisma's eyes began to sting at the memory of the time she last saw Ivan.

"Honey, what's going on with you? You're treating me so coldly. I'm not the enemy. I'm not the one who hurt you. If anything, I have always been there for you."

"I'm not asking you to be there for me, Ivan! I wanted a relationship with you, not a one-sided charity case, and that's all I am to you right now!"

"What?! A charity case? Is that how you think I see you, Charisma?"

"Yes, that's how I KNOW you see me. You got so far caught up in this relationship that now you probably feel stuck and obligated to hang around. But let me tell you something, I'm a strong woman. I don't need your sympathy! I came here alone, watched my mom die, was raped and everything else bad that can happen to a young girl is probably going to happen to me. Why would you want to hang around for the ride?"

"You know, Charisma, I'm about tired of your pity party. Yes, your mom died and yes, MY homie died too. We both been through some shit!"

"Yeah, but were you raped, Ivan?! Did a sick bastard take advantage of you? No, I don't think so. So, I suggest you just get out of my face!"

Ivan just stood there frozen. Charisma's words cut him deep. He knew she was in pain but the reality of that pain became much more real now.

"Baby, I'm so sorry. Come here," he said, walking over to her with his arms open wide.

"Don't come any closer to me!" She snapped.

"Charisma, it's me," Ivan said, feeling shot down and confused.

"So now you think I'm stupid? I know who you are. We were only having a conversation for the past two hours. We only spent six hours at the hospital together. Yet you feel the need to tell me who you are?" She quipped at him sarcastically.

Still walking toward her, Ivan said, "Baby, come here. Let me hold you, you're hurting. That's all this is. You just need someone to lean on right now. Please, Charisma, just let me be there for you."

Charisma paused for a moment and really debated giving in. She wanted so badly to fold into his strong arms. Looking into his eyes, she felt his care for her and began to give up when almost out of nowhere, she had a memory of the night at Franky's house.

Right before her eyes, it was like a movie playing in front of her. She could see Franky standing over her and buckling his pants then walking away.

The next thing she knew, she saw darkness.

CHAPTER TWENTY-FOUR
IT'S STILL GOODBYE

"Honey! Honey! Please wake up, Charisma, please wake up, baby!" Ivan had Charisma in his arms patting her cheeks desperately trying to wake her up.

Charisma opened her eyes and looked up to see Ivan's face. Relieved it wasn't Franky's again, like she'd just seen a while ago, she asked, "what happened?"

"I don't know. We were talking and out of nowhere you just passed out. Luckily, I caught you or you would have hit your head on the side of the counter."

She looked around and realized she was lying in Ivan's arms on the sofa. Charisma tried to sit herself up.

"How do you feel?" Ivan asked.

"Like I've just been run over by a truck."

"Want me to get you some water?"

"No, but I think I'd like it if you left though."

"Really, Charisma? Are we back on this again?"

"I never left it."

"If I wasn't here just now you could have really hurt yourself on that corner," he shot back.

"But you were, and I thank you for your help, Ivan. But I'm no good for you. You and I both know this," she pleaded with her face in her hands.

"No, Charisma, only YOU know this. What I know is that I love you, and I want to be with you and help you. Not because you are a charity case but because that's what people do when they love each other."

Charisma looked up immediately. She had never heard him say that he loved her before. He had always insinuated it, but never came out and said it.

"But I'm not going to continue to beg for someone's love that doesn't want me nor love me back." Ivan walked over to the door and opened it. Without turning around he said, "goodbye, Charisma. Good luck, and I pray that you will be safe."

That was the last time Charisma had seen or heard from Ivan. She sat on that couch for what seemed like hours and cried her eyes out. After all he had done for her, what right did she have to treat him that way? She questioned herself but already knew the answer. Charisma was protecting him... protecting him from... herself.

It began to rain outside, and the apartment began to get dark. Charisma lay curled up on the couch staring out into the overcast sky. She remembered there was a time when she absolutely loved rainy days. She would sit on the windowsill in her room and lean up against the window to get as close to the rain as possible and just write. She used to love the cool feel of the air on her cheek as she pressed it against the glass. Sometimes she would even open the window a little to breathe in the fresh smell of the rain. How great it used to make her feel.

The inspiration that she used to get from the vibration of the thunder was so beautiful. But nowadays nothing inspires her. Charisma felt like she couldn't write anything if her life depended on it right now.

She got up and went into her bedroom and opened the drawer that used to be her mother's. She dug through the mounds of medication that filled her drawer next to the bed. Ever since her mother died, she would occasionally take the sleeping pills.

Recently, more frequently, she started taking the ones marked Vicodin. She made sure to stay very clear of the ecstasy pills but today she really didn't care. What was she living for? With one of the pills in her hand, Charisma headed into the kitchen and swallowed it down with a glass of water.

Looking around the apartment, Charisma felt so alone. *Why? Why did I make him leave? He was my only friend, all I had. Charisma, you are really getting stupid. What's happening to you?*

She laid out on the couch waiting for her newfound drug to kick in. She found herself rubbing her hands on the sofa. It was so amazingly soft. She had never noticed the soft texture of this couch before. She was all of a sudden infatuated with the feel of the couch.

She sat up to get a good look at the material. As she ran her hands across the cushions, she felt something rough in between them. She pulled out a folded piece of paper. Opening it, she realized it was something written by her mother. Her high was immediately put on hold as she looked over the letter.

The very first thing Charisma noticed was the letter was written in poetry form. Surprised by this, Charisma wished now more than ever that she would have had more time to get to know her mother. Now she understood herself just a little better all of a sudden.

"My mother was also a writer?" she thought to herself. It pained her to know she never got to share some of her work with her.

Charisma tried to imagine her mother in this same apartment, sitting here in this very spot, on a gloomy day like this. Imagined what her mother would have felt, looking out this same window that she was looking out right now, watching the rain begin to pour down. She took a deep breath and read her mother's words:

I made a mistake that I will always regret.
One that I know I can never forget.
Went out with my friends, expected some fun.
Did something else instead,
Did something real dumb.

I swallowed a pill that made me high.
I'm not sure when and I don't know why.

I guess I thought it would take away my stress,
Throw away my problems and give me the best.

Now I know, I know I was wrong.
I know too late, but at least I'm not gone.

I remember in the car, my heart beating fast,
Faster and faster,
I didn't think I would last.

I cried and I pleaded for just one more chance,
I begged the one with my life in his hands.

As I reminded him of my baby,
How she needed me,
He slowly let go and set my heart free.

My friend slapped my face and told me to breathe,
I could see the fear in her eyes.
She didn't want me to leave.

I thank God for this friend who was there for me that night,
Because all my other friends were out of sight.
Things sometimes change like a fad or a trend,
But one thing remains the same,
That's a true and real best friend.

Love you, Sophie.

Charisma slid down to the floor, leaned her head against the sofa, and cried for her mother. She cried so hard she couldn't breathe.

Why did you leave me? Why, momma?! I have so many questions to ask you. Why? I need you so badly right now. Please! She cried out to no one in the room. Charisma held the poem to her chest and sat alone on the floor and just cried.

*****

Cherry's excited voice pulled her out of those memories. She heard her saying, "Yeah, girl, I think that goes fabulous together. Looking down, she realized she was standing in front of a mirror all dressed up. She was in the skimpiest outfit she'd ever seen. And in the highest heels she'd ever put on her feet. Charisma was so deep in thought she had completely forgotten that she was at the mall shopping with Cherry for clothes for her new scandalous profession.

"So, do you want it?"

"What?"

"Do you want it?"

"Want what?" Charisma asked, still a little dazed from her daydreaming.

"The outfit, girl. I'm trying to move on quickly so we can get you some food, hun."

"Oh...yeah...this. Yeah, it'll do I guess."

"Okay, well change so we can go pay for it and head down to the food court. I'll wait for you out here."

"Okay," Charisma said, glancing at herself one last time in the mirror.

Back in the dressing room, Charisma changed with her back to the mirror. She didn't want to see herself again. She just wanted to get out of here and get back home but knew this wasn't the case for her.

She knew this was the beginning of a new chapter for her. One that she knew she would very soon regret.

CHAPTER TWENTY-FIVE
FIRST DANCE

"Next out tonight, gentlemen, is a newbie to the Scarlett Letter!" Let's welcome, Suuuunfloweeeeer....!

Charisma walked out onto the stage with her silver see-through skirt, bikini top and heels that made her feel extra tall and uncomfortable. She did everything that Cherry taught her, even down to the spins. The nervousness she felt, left the moment she walked out on the stage. Instead, she felt a thrill of excitement as the music boomed through her body.

Every step she took, she could feel the music. Her body automatically moved in sync with every beat almost on its own. She never had to think of her next move, it came as natural as her breathing. Charisma became entranced by the way the men looked at her and at the same time, entranced them.

She walked slowly to the center of the stage and stared directly into the eyes of a man who had been sitting toward the front of the club. His friends were talking to him, but she could see she had all his attention. She continued closer toward the end of the stage, staring directly into the strangers' eyes as she moved across the front of the stage. As the song came to an end, she gathered her things, walked toward the curtains, and slightly turned her head toward the stranger and gave him a quick glance.

"Oh, my goodness Charisma! That was amazing!" All the girls in the back crowded around her.

One of the girls asked, "Are you sure that was your first time ever on stage?"

Another said, "Did you see how everyone's mouths dropped when she walked out there?"

Cherry excitedly chimed in with the accolades. "Girl, you had that one dude eating out the palm of your hand!!"

As all the girls were chattering, Charisma couldn't get the strangers' face out of her head. The thought of the way he looked at her left a hurtful feeling in her gut. She had never seen a man look at her in this way before. The thought that the only way a man could ever look at her in such a way was if she were strutting across a stage half naked made her sad.

At home that night, Charisma continued to think about this stranger. She couldn't seem to shake the way his eyes moved over her body. It didn't make her feel good like the girls would have believed. She actually felt ashamed... Ashamed of what she was doing. Of where she was. Of *who* she had become.

But who was he? She asked herself. *Who was he to judge her anyway? If anything, he should be ashamed of himself for even being there. He knew why he was there. He knew what kind of club this was, and he would probably be back there again...*

The thought of that sent a thrill through her body. The thought of actually seeing this stranger again excited her in a way she hadn't felt in a long time. As she was fixing a cup of tea, she asked herself, *"what is it with this guy? Why can't I shake him?"*

Charisma took her teacup and her poetry book and sat out by her window. She opened it to let the cool, after rain breeze flow into the apartment. The smell of the recent rain filled the apartment and gave her a warm feeling despite the cool air. She held her warm cup of tea in the palm of her hands, curled up next to the window, and continued to breathe in the fresh air.

Charisma's mind trailed back to last night at the club; the fear she had right as they called her onto the stage. The way her legs shook as she tried to walk onto the stage in those very high heels. She remembered the calming she felt as she became one with the music. The way she closed her eyes and felt free as she spun around the pole. To get herself through the moment, she told herself she was swinging on a swing at the park like she used to do as a child.

Cherry and the other girls taught Charisma all the tricks. She learned very quickly and was comfortable even on her first time out on the stage. She knew how to turn herself upside down on the pole then right side up again. She knew how to make her body swing faster, then slow down again to match the beat of the music. Charisma was a natural.

In her memory, *she could see his eyes on her as she locked hers with his. She could feel the burning between the two of them. The strange connection they had as if no one else existed in the room but the two of them. She needed to get closer to see him, so she slowly walked to the edge of the stage.*

She stared; he stared back. They never blinked. She could see the mouth of his friends moving, but he never took his eyes from her, nor her from him...then the song stopped.

Charisma looked out at the cloudy skies as her heart pounded at the memory. "What is wrong with me?" She scolded herself.

"All dogs. These men are all dogs. He's probably married and going to the club without her even knowing. He's probably hurt and lied to many women and is now at the Scarlett Letter looking for someone else to hurt. It won't be me. I tell you that right now, it will not be me."

She took a sip of her hot tea and decided to journal. Charisma always allowed her heart to lead her through her writing.

This man...so beautiful in every way. This man... his eyes so strong and so bold they make me shiver. The gorgeous shape of almonds sitting on his beautifully chiseled face. His eyes, the color of coal... so dark, so mischievous, yet so innocent and lovingly burns a hole through my soul. I would get lost in his glare. His skin... the color of midnight, I would love to feel the smooth touch of his cheek close to my face. To smell his breath as he breathes into my mouth, and I inhale his every word. I want him...

Why? Why does this man intrigue me so? He looks up at me, he watches me, and I know he sees me as less than a human. As if I am no good to mankind because of where and who I am. I know he watches me for his own pleasure and thinks nothing more of me but as legs, butt, and breasts. Who is he to judge me?... He is beauty... He is magnificent, but me... I am just me.

I used to be better than this. Used to be a woman worthwhile. Used to be a woman worthy of a man like him... but now...now I am just who I am.

How did I get here? Where did I make my wrong turn in life?

One day, a beautiful young girl with the whole world at my feet and now... now, I bow before the world asking it to be easy on me. Begging for it to give me a break. Fighting for life, for air.

I've been searching for love in all the wrong places. Now I have found love at first sight and this man is too good for me. When did I become this woman? I degrade myself before him as his eyes rape me. What else would I expect?

This man. This man, he is beauty, and me...me… I used to be...

CHAPTER TWENTY – SIX
MY NAME IS MICHAEL

The next night at work, Charisma mingled throughout the club as she was taught. She smiled and laughed with the men pretending to be interested in what they had to say. She easily became annoyed because no one ever asked about her. They all wanted to talk about themselves and stare at her, which got old to her very quickly.

The one good thing she could find was that this was not a nude club. They all wore bathing suits, heels, and skimpy skirts. That's how she got herself through each night; telling herself that this was no different than walking on the beach.

Just as she was heading to the back for a break from this awful feeling of men just glaring at her, she saw him...the stranger. There he was, sitting at a table, with a drink but this time he was alone. Just as the other men were doing, he was staring at her, but his gaze was a little more peculiar.

"Can I help you?" She sashayed up to his table with a pretend boldness to try hard to stay in character.

"Excuse me?" The man responded with a confused look on his face.

"You can play dumb all you want. We both know that you have been watching me since the last time you were here."

"Really? Because if you noticed me watching you, then who is watching who?" The man said with a slight grin.

"You most definitely know what I mean," Charisma retorted, now feeling very irritated by this stranger. He almost seemed to be picking on her. Almost laughing at her expense, and she wasn't in the mood for it.

"And, if I can add another thing, it seems to me that there are many people in this room WATCHING as you call it. I don't see you questioning anyone else."

Instantly, Charisma felt a bit silly for harassing this man. What came over her? Is this not a strip club? Weren't all the men in here watching them? What made her question him this way?

"I…I'm sorry…. I'm not sure what I was thinking in that moment. I'll leave you alone." She turned to walk off feeling confused about what had just happened.

"No, please. Sit," the man said.

Reluctantly, Charisma sat across from the man at the high-top round table. For a while, they didn't speak. He just sipped his drink and every so often, glanced in her direction.

"So, what you drinking?" She was feeling so awkward and just needed to have some kind of conversation going.

"Pepsi."

Charisma belted out a hardy laugh that caught the man off guard. "Pepsi," she repeated. "Yeah right!"

"Here, taste it for yourself."

As Charisma put the cup to her face, she very well expected to just sniff the glass and smell the liquor in the cup but there was no smell. Her curiosity got the best of her, and she took a sip. Only to find that the man was telling the truth. He was only drinking Pepsi.

"Why?" She asked in confusion.

"Why, what?"

"Why would you come to a place like this to only drink Pepsi? I don't understand."

"Oh. Well, I'm working so it's best for me to stay soberminded."

"Working?" She scoffed at him. "So are all these other men in here but it doesn't stop none of them."

"Yeah, well my job may be different from these guys. Maybe I take my work a little more seriously."

"What is your work?" Charisma asked, giving a slight chuckle.

"I teach."

"What?"

"Many things."

"Like what?"

"I show people how to be successful in their occupation. How to make better choices and grow in their field of expertise."

"Oh, like a recruiter?"

"Something like that. It's my job to help people find their way, and I take that very seriously."

All of a sudden, Charisma's attention went to his left wrist. He was wearing a gray wrist band that had the letters WWJD written across it.

"What does that mean?" She asked.

"My band? It stands for What Would Jesus Do?"

Charisma felt a sudden rush of warmth rise up through her. She could tell she was turning red. Her skin was beginning to feel clammy and damp. She felt as though she might very well pass out.

"Charisma, are you okay?" The strange man asked her.

"I never told you my real name."

"I know."

"Who are you? Why are you in this club sporting a Jesus anything?!" Charisma asked, almost yelling at this point.

"Are you more upset that I'm in this club or that I'm in this club with my Jesus bracelet on?" He asked her with the same know it all smile he had the first time she saw him. Before she could respond to him, he asked her another question. "Are you walking in your calling?"

Charisma felt her body get warm. She noticed that the people in the room were all still having their respective conversations. However, she couldn't hear anything but her heart beating in her ears. She looked across the small high-top table at this strange man as he questioned her.

"I don't understand your question."

"Oh, but I'm sure you do," the stranger retorted before she could even think. "Are you walking in the calling that is over your life? Is this what you were called to do?"

"Listen, you don't get to come here and judge me!" Charisma nearly shouted to the stranger from across the table.

"What makes you think I'm judging you? I just asked a question. A simple yes or no would suffice."

Charisma sat in frustration staring at him. She didn't know what to say or do. She didn't know how to respond to his question.

She even began to feel lightheaded again. Something that had been happening more and more lately. Charisma attributed it to her newfound experimentation with her mother's old pills. She was pretty sure those had everything to do with her groggy feelings lately. But Charisma knew it was the only way she was going to get through each night undressing in front of strangers. It was the one thing that took the edge off and allowed her to step into her alter ego of "Sunflower." These pills made her feel invincible, bold, powerful. Like she could take on anything that came her way...except this.

Something about this man was stopping her buzz and making her see clearer which is NOT what Charisma wanted. She wanted to numb the pain of her not living the life her parents prayed for her to have. Yet here she was in full view, realizing what a mess she'd made of herself and her life. Thanks to this stranger who had the audacity to invade her life and dredge up all these unwanted emotions.

"Who are you and what do you want?" Charisma asked boldly.

"I want nothing, Charisma. I'm just having innocent conversation."

"And that's another thing. How do you know my name? No one here gives anyone our real names. The only name you should know me as is Sunflower. So, again, I ask you - How do you know my name?"

"I'm here for you."

"For me?!" She shouted.

"Yes, for you. Charisma, it's time to be still. You're going to need to be still and listen to God. Like really get to know Him. He's waiting for you to come back to Him."

"Are you seriously in here giving me a sermon on how I need to go back to church?"

"I never said anything about going back to church. I said go back to Him," the stranger said matter of factly.

The room began to spin; Charisma felt dizzy. She became nervous that this stranger somehow slipped something in her drink. She tried to wave her hands to Cherry who was walking by, but Cherry assumed she was just being playful with the man at the table. She waved back at her as she walked by.

Charisma could not speak. No words would come out of her mouth as she began to fall unconscious. As she was falling, she felt the stranger grab her. He carried her to a nearby couch. As he carried her, she heard him whisper in her ear.

"Charisma, you're carrying a child. He is very special. Don't take any more pills that could be harmful to your body and the baby. Do not become bitter because of the man that hurt you. The baby belongs to the Lord, not him. It's time to walk in your calling and allow God to change you from the inside out. This baby needs you and he needs you in sound mind."

Charisma was able to get out a muster and asked, "Who are you? What is your name?" She felt her body being set down on the couch in the front entry way of the club. Her eyes could barely stay open as she tried to keep her gaze locked in on the stranger. He swiftly bent down and whispered softly in her ear. Michael… My name is Michael."

Then she was out. Charisma had passed out cold. Right there in the club, on the couch, in front of the entry way.

CHAPTER TWENTY - SEVEN
IT'S TIME TO GO HOME

"Charisma! Charisma! Charisma, girl, please wake up!" Her friend, Cherry, begged as she dabbed a wet washcloth on her face and forehead.

Charisma finally woke up from what felt like a crazy dream. It was good for her to open her eyes and see a familiar face in Cherry.

"Girl, do you have any juice in this fridge so I can get you something to drink?" Cherry shouted out from the kitchen, rummaging through the fridge.

"What happened?" Charisma asked, trying to sit up. "I feel so dizzy."

"Girl, you literally just passed out in the middle of The Scarlett in front of everyone."

"I did?" Charisma tried so hard to remember what took place that night, when she remembered the stranger she was talking to in the club. "What was his name again?" She tried to think. "Michael! That's it, Michael!"

"What are you mumbling about over there, Charisma?"

"The man in the club I was talking to. His name was Michael."

"Ohh Kaay, there's plenty of Michael's, Charisma. What makes this one so special, honey?" Cherry complained, stroking her friend's hair, and trying to sit her up to drink some apple juice.

"To be honest, Charisma, his real name may not even be Michael," she laughed. "You know that's a make-believe world in there anyway. No names are real; no one gives their real name in The Scarlett."

Charisma just sat there sipping her apple juice trying to process what she was feeling. There was still something hovering over her, and she couldn't figure it out. Why was she feeling like something was looming? Then it hit her! "Cherry, what did you say about people knowing names?"

"What? You mean that no one knows anyone's real name in The Scarlett? It's true. The Scarlett is a fantasy world. No one knows who you are there."

"But that's just it, Cherry. The stranger knew my name."

"What? How?"

"I don't know." Charisma looked down at her tummy wondering about what else she remembered him say, and wondering if she should tell Cherry. "He also said something else to me before I went out," Charisma said quietly.

"What?" Cherry asked with strong inquisition at this point.

"He... he told me that I was carrying a baby boy."

"What?!" Cherry laughed as she responded. "You don't actually believe his nonsense do you, Charisma?"

"I mean…"

"Charisma, please tell me you don't actually believe him. He's just another one of the many storyteller men that walk in, feeding off our emotions, and thinking we are stupid enough to fall for it."

Charisma looked down in embarrassment. She could not respond to her friend.

"Charisma, I'm sorry sweetie. I'm not saying you're stupid, love. I'm just saying you're new to the game. These men come in all the time with this mess, and we have to stay guarded. We can't take in everything they say."

"Cherry, I did pass out."

"So, what! You've been drinking," she snapped.

"Cherry, would you listen to me?"

"Charisma, I've listened to this mess long enough. You cannot take in what these guys say. What do you think he is? Some kind of psychic or something?"

"No. I think he might have been my angel," Charisma said, then quickly regretted it.

"You mean as in your guardian angel?"

Charisma nods slowly.

"Sweetie, come here." Cherry flops on the couch and hugs her friend as she begins to cry uncontrollably.

"Charisma, what's going on, honey? What makes you think this random stranger is your guardian angel?"

Charisma was so grateful for this moment with her friend. To have someone hold her the way her mom, Lena, used to hold her as a young girl, whenever she would come home from school after a fight with her best friend. Her mom would always hug her tight and let her lean on her shoulder as she cried into her neck.

"He said I'm carrying a baby boy," Charisma blubbered. "Cherry, I was raped a few months ago by my mom's old friend Franky," she said, bawling into her friend's neck. In that moment, Charisma let it all out.

"Charisma, what in the world are you saying to me? What monster did this to you? We need to take you to the hospital. We need to press charges. There's so much that needs to be done right now." Cherry began to scramble to grab her purse and Charisma's shoes.

"Cherry, stop! I've already done all of that. This was months ago. I've gone to the hospital. They did all they needed to do."

"Did they test you for…"

"Yes! They tested me for everything."

"AND?!"

"And I'm fine… Or as fine as I can be," Charisma said, looking down and playing with her fingers.

"Well, if they tested for everything, then what's this about a baby boy?"

"It would have been too soon for a pregnancy to show up, Cherry. Ivan took me to the hospital the same night it happened to me. There's no way doctors could have possibly seen that back then."

"So, what's the plan now?"

"Well, I'm going to confirm this pregnancy. Then make some changes. Cherry, this baby didn't ask for the life I have given myself. Everything that has happened to me thus far, I chose, and I realize that now. It wouldn't be so bad if it were just me, but it's not anymore.

"Charisma, you sound as if you already know for sure that you're pregnant, and you don't!"

"I do!! Cherry, look, none of this needs to make sense to you. Heck, it barely makes sense to me, but I know what I know.

I grew up in the church all my life, and I've been running from God since I got here. Nothing has been good. NOTHING. I see it now. I don't know what I thought I was searching for coming here but I know one thing. I was searching on my own and without God. All I found was chaos.

Yes, I found out the truth about my birth mom, but maybe it wasn't meant for me to know. All it did was spiral me out of control. My mom was the one who actually raised me, loved me, and cared for me all my life. All they wanted was to protect me from the pains and hurts of this world and I still found a way to go out and find it.

I didn't know my cousin was actually my mother. I still don't know who my real father is. But again, Cherry, none of that matters. I had the best family ever back home. They loved and cared for me. This…this isn't love.

What I'm living here is pure torture. I'm not doing this to my son. I'm not letting him live the life I lived this past year. I'm going back. I'm going back home where I belong."

"Charisma, you're going to give up all this, girl? Just because you think you're pregnant and some man in a club spit some lame game in your ear?"

As Cherry was reprimanding her, Charisma remembered something. Not only did God send her an angel in the club, but the taxi driver was also speaking into her life and Ivan had been around to help her when she was in trouble. Heck, why not go all the way back to her childhood and acknowledge Lena and her dad who lovingly took her as their own?

God had set up her whole life with angels. People to guide, protect, and help her every step of the way. In that moment, Charisma was so grateful to God for it all that she had a smile on her face.

"Charisma, are you even listening to me? What are you over here smiling about anyway?"

"Yes."

"Yes, what?" Cherry retorted, frustrated.

"You asked if I was willing to give all this up." Charisma looked around the beautiful, spacious apartment and smiled again.

"The answer is yes, I'm ready. So ready. I wanna go home."

CHAPTER TWENTY - EIGHT
BACK TO THE BEGINNING

"Hey, girl! Girl, wake up! We done stopped. You better get off now if you tryna go use the restroom or go get you something to eat. We ain't stoppin' again 'til we reach Naples!" Charisma smiled as she knew she was almost home. She couldn't wait to see her mom and dad again and wrap her arms tightly around them.

The past five months had been a doozy getting her mom's place in order and packing up all her belongings to have shipped back home. It didn't help that she had the worst morning sickness ever known to woman or so she thought. Her morning sickness was so bad she had lost 20 pounds and Charisma wasn't that big of a girl to begin with.

She had gotten so skinny because she could barely keep down food. At three months pregnant, she looked five months. Now at five months pregnant, Charisma is showing like a seven-month belly.

Charisma noticed the pitiful look on the driver's face as she got up to leave the bus. She ignored it and realized she didn't owe anyone an explanation about her life. He could think whatever he wanted. One thing she knew was she was back on the right track and was proud of herself.

Charisma had enrolled in online classes and after having the baby, she planned to register for the local school in her small town to get her degree in ministry. This time out here in the big city had been a journey for her. Not something that she would take again if she knew sooner what the journey entailed. But there were some good lessons that came from it all and she found God in it in a way she had never seen Him before.

Charisma realized that what the enemy meant for evil in her life, God was always around making sure she was safe. Making sure everything worked out for her good.

CHAPTER TWENTY - NINE
I'M HOME

"Charisma!!" She heard her mom and dad shout out her name. Charisma spun around to see them running toward her with tears in their eyes. In this moment, Charisma was reminded of the story, The Prodigal Son. She remembered that although the son left home and made such terrible choices in life, he was welcomed home with open arms and real, true love from his father.

Although Charisma attended church weekly, with her mom and dad, including Sunday school, she did not read her bible much as a kid. However, she did know many of the bible characters. She just never knew them as in depth and personally as she did now.

The Bible had become her favorite book to read so the characters had become like friends and family to her. They were all she had during this time. In her last few months in New York, while preparing to return home, she read the bible daily. When she couldn't read it, she played it on recordings.

Charisma was very excited about her new outlook on life. Ever since she turned her life over to God, it's like everything completely changed. Nothing was perfect, of course. She still had a few run-ins with Franky and had to deal with that and the police. But she was strong and did everything the courts asked her to do and Franky was convicted of rape.

Charisma knew that most women would probably abort this child but that was never an option for her. What the enemy meant for evil; God would use for good. This child was going to do great things for the kingdom of God.

Oh, and yes, Charisma's hunch that she was carrying a boy was accurate. The ultrasound showed a healthy baby boy. Ready and reared to come into this world and change some things for the better.

Charisma's mom and dad hugged her tightly and didn't let go for what seemed like an eternity. Charisma was completely okay with that. She needed this love so badly and was happy to be safe in her mom and dad's arms.

"I'm home," she whispered. "I'm home."

"Charisma, let's get you home and get some food in your body. Baby, you are skin and bones!" Her mother fussed over her. She felt a little embarrassed by the comment but knew her mom meant it from a good place of love.

"Mom! I have a lot of fat right here in this belly of mine," she giggled, holding her tummy, and smiling.

"Yes, and that little guy is sucking all the nutrition from MY baby girl. We are going to have to put some food in ya' young lady," her mom said, pulling her close and kissing her on her forehead.

On the ride home, Charisma's dad could not stop smiling. She could see him constantly checking on her in the rearview mirror. As if he was making sure she was still in the back seat.

"I ain't going nowhere, daddy," Charisma said with a smile the last time he looked back at her from the mirror.

"I know, baby. It's just so surreal to see you sitting back there again. The last time was when we were taking you to the airport, and now here you are again. Charisma, your mom and I just want you to know we trust our God and not what our eyes see."

"What do you mean, daddy?"

"What I'm saying is, the world may look at you and think they already know the ending to your story just by seeing you pregnant and maybe hearing some of what you've experienced out there in New York. But, baby, don't let the naysayers rob you of your joy or of what God has for you. The devil comes to steal, kill, and destroy and he tried with you, but he did not succeed. You hear me?"

"Yes sir."

"He did NOT win! Your mom and I have been praying over you since the day you left and have never missed a day."

"I have specifically prayed that God would send his angels to protect, watch, and keep you through your journey," said Charisma's mom.

In that moment, Charisma remembered the few encounters that she had and kept so dear to her heart. All she could think was, *"thank you, mommy. For praying for me. It worked. God heard you. He never left me, and he did send angels to guard me. Actually a few,"* she thought as she continued to look out the window at all the familiar sites she had been used to as a child.

It felt so good to be home. This was going to be her next chapter.

CHAPTER THIRTY
THE PROPHECY

Charisma remembered while in New York she searched for a church to go to one Wednesday night. She remembered a church on the corner that she would walk by on the way to work some nights. She would always feel joy in her heart when she walked by and heard them singing. So, she took a little stroll down 7th St. As always, she could hear the beautiful sound coming from this church. This time, she walked in.

Charisma creeped in slowly and sat in the back. She noticed the beautiful look of this old church. The organs and the pipes that went up the walls were so impressive and majestic. The people were singing and clapping and were so happy in there. It made her feel like she belonged. To be honest, this church reminded her of her little church back home.

She sat and rocked back and forth and allowed the music to engulf her. It was as if the Holy Spirit was right there in that moment with her. As if He came down from heaven and was circling about her with a warmth that she hadn't felt before. The feeling was so mesmerizing that she didn't realize that the choir had stopped singing. For her, the music in her head was still going. Charisma was so at peace that she didn't realize they had begun the teaching already.

Charisma listened as the preacher taught on acceptance. He talked about how we so badly want to be so accepted by the world that we tend to put aside the Word and its directions. This teaching was so spot on that Charisma had tears in her eyes. After the teaching, a man in a green tie walked up and took the mic. She heard them refer to this man as Prophet Brown.

Prophet Brown took one step to the podium and looked directly at Charisma. Her heart began to beat in her chest. She didn't know why, but all of a sudden, she felt an urgency.

"Young lady," Prophet Brown said very sternly into the mic.

Charisma looked at him with confusion as he confirmed her doubts and called out to her but this time pointing directly at her. "Young lady, stand up, will you please?"

Charisma slowly stood up and looked around at the small crowd of people in the church. Unsure of what was going to happen next.

A sweet lady from behind her softly touched her shoulder and told her, "go head, baby. Stand up. The man of God has a word for you." Charisma turned to face her and saw her sweet smile and felt at peace. Then she turned back around to face whatever was about to be said by this man.

"Young lady, the hand of the Lord is on you. His favor is over you and your life."

Charisma could hear the lady behind her whispering, "Jesus, Jesus, Jesus." She heard a few amens throughout the church but wasn't sure what she was supposed to say for herself in that moment. She then realized the man was not finished.

"You are about to encounter a very new season. As you walk it, walk it with bravery. The valley of the shadow of death is great, but God is greater. On this journey, when you become afraid, remember the Word says God does not give us a spirit of fear. He gives us a sound mind and clarity. So, when fear creeps in, you must know that is from the enemy. Rebuke it!! Rebuke it immediately each time and speak the word of God over yourself.

If you do not have the word of God fully in your arsenal, change that immediately. Get in the Word and begin to memorize scripture so that you can have it at opportune times.

Don't be caught off guard by the wiles of the enemy! Start with Genesis and read…READ! Take notes. You will write. You will write so much that journals will fill, and you will have to find new ones.

I see God's word written in your notes, in your journals, and on your heart. You will fill yourself so much with His word, the enemy will fear you. You will set fear to the spirit of fear. You will become so bold you will set anxiety to the spirit of anxiety.

Read Exodus. Become familiar with that book. The people were under slavery and were set free. God has set you free. What you thought was news that was going to tie you down more emotionally, was news you needed. You needed that reality because now you can move on with the truth. This didn't hold you back. It set you free. All that happened was all part of the story you will tell to now help free other women. It's no longer YOUR story. It's HIS story and HIS glory will come from it all.

Be faithful, trust Him, and know He means you well. He has sent many to protect you on this journey and to show you, you're never alone. The people He has sent are to light your path in this dark world. Think of them as little fireflies. As you see them, turn, and go in that direction.

Walk in faith because soon the next one will appear letting you know which way to go next. They are your signals in which to light your path as you go. Like illuminating steps that mark your path.

Pay attention to the smallest of details. God is in the details. He speaks to you. Pay close attention because our Father has a still voice. You need to still yourself in meditation to catch it. Your prayer should always be, Lord, let me not miss you in this day. God means you well. Your latter days will be better than your former days, thus says the Lord."

Charisma felt wind rushing over her and was overwhelmed by the feeling. She looked around the church and saw hands stretched toward her in prayer. People were praying in a tongue she didn't understand but felt. She knew they were all praying blessings over her, and she received each and every one of their prayers.

After the service, the woman behind her softly spoke to her. "That was a powerful word spoken over you tonight. I hope you go home and write it all down so you can refer to it later."

"Yes ma'am. I plan to do exactly that. Thank you."

"Alright, well goodnight. Hope to see you here again. It was a blessing having you worship with us this evening. Don't be a stranger," she shouted as she waved goodbye.

Charisma bent down to grab her bag from the pew and turned to thank the nice woman and say goodbye. When she looked for her, she was gone. Charisma thought to herself, *how could that be? She could not have gone far at all. The woman was just standing here.*

As she began her walk home, she couldn't help thinking about the sweet woman who seemed to have disappeared into thin air.

CHAPTER THIRTY - ONE
HE BELONGS TO GOD

"AHHHHHH!!!" screamed Charisma.

"It hurts so bad! God, please help me! This hurts so bad, please God help me!!"

Charisma's mom held her hand on one side of the hospital bed. Meanwhile, her dad paced outside the door, hearing his little girl scream in pain.

"Charisma, I need you to listen to me and listen closely," the doctor said with urgency, looking over his thick glasses. "When I say push, I need you to push with all your might."

"I can't!"

"Yes, you can!" He shouted back at her from the bottom of the hospital bed, ready to catch the baby.

"It hurts too bad, and I'm scared!"

"Charisma, your baby's life depends on YOU right now. He's losing oxygen and we need to get him out NOW! I need you to muster up whatever strength you've got, from wherever it can come from, and I need you to PUSH!"

The moment Charisma heard that her son's life may be in danger, she forgot all about her pain. She was laser focused on getting him out and breathing. She remembered the pastor who told her, "God never gave you a spirit of fear. So, when you feel afraid, recognize where that feeling is coming from. A wave of strength showered over Charisma, and she pushed like her life depended on it. In reality, her son's life did depend on it.

She pushed as she shouted out, "You can't have my son!! He belongs to God!!" And just like that, he was out and crying.

The sound of his wailing filled the room. It was the most beautiful sound she had ever heard. Her dad came in ecstatic and went straight to Charisma and hugged her tight. He whispered, "I prayed for you baby girl. I prayed so hard for you out there."

"I know you did daddy. I know and thank you. It helped me so much. He's so beautiful."

Charisma's father looked at him and began to cry. "Thank you, baby girl. Thank you for coming back home and bringing such a special gift back with you. Look at what God has done," her father said as he wiped a tear from his eyes.

"What's his name?"

"I don't know yet."

"You don't know? Sweetie, you've only had 9 months to think about the name of your first child." Her dad lightheartedly teased as he leaned over and kissed her on the forehead.

"I know, daddy, but there's just so many names out there and I don't want just any name for him. He's so special and the way he came into this world is also significant. I know God has a special name for him that He will give me when the time is right."

"Well, your mother and I know how strong willed you are, so we are not here to change your mind on this name thing. We can only pray that you hear God's name for him before you have to leave this hospital." Her Dad winked at her before leaving the room to go down and grab a bite to eat from the cafeteria.

"Get some rest, ladybug. I'll be back in a little."

"Okay, dad! Thanks!"

CHAPTER THIRTY - TWO
IT IS WELL

The next morning, Charisma woke up in a daze, realizing it was a new day, and she was a mother. She looked around the hospital room and took in the memory of the night prior.

She remembered laboring with her baby from home to the hospital. She remembered being in her old room at her parents' house and just being so happy to be back home. She had sat on her windowsill to watch the rain as she had so often done in the past as a child, to a young girl, even in her teens. She would sit on that very windowsill of her bedroom and look out at the rain. It was always her favorite thing to do.

Charisma was always told she was a water baby. Water in any form brought her so much happiness. But rain… rain brought her peace. Especially a good storm going on outside; she was in heaven.

People always found that strange about her. While everyone else was panicking about a storm coming, Charisma would have bouts of excitement and adrenalin running through her. She would look forward to the storm.

Well, that particular evening, her and her family had just had the most amazing celebration. The ladies from the church had put on a baby shower for Charisma. Everyone at Emmanuel Baptist Church had been so understanding, loving, and kind to her through the whole ordeal. No one seemed to look down on her or treat her badly. It was one of the biggest things Charisma feared. How was she going to be looked at by the church? The answer was with love.

Charisma was looked at with nothing but love. It's such a beautiful thing when you have a family who takes you in regardless of your mistake. They knew her heart and knew how upset she already was with herself for the choices she had made while away in the big city.

She had chosen to speak while she was still pregnant at one of the sisters' prayer breakfast. She spoke about choices and how the choices you make in life determine your path. There were quite a few of the younger girls at this prayer breakfast than in the past and she knew why, along with everyone else. They had never really had anyone at the church openly experience something like Charisma's story and word had gotten around fast about her experiences. It didn't help that Charisma was also very vocal herself.

Her goal was to share as much as she could to help anyone and everyone not make the same mistakes she had made. Charisma was on a mission to help open the eyes of young girls, being blinded by the glitz and glamour of what the TV showed them about the fast-paced life. She was on a mission to pull the cover off the devil and expose him fully, even if it meant embarrassment for herself.

She felt it was the least sacrifice she could make for God saving her from whatever life could have been. She knew the little she experienced was nowhere near what the enemy had in store for her life. The enemy's plot against her was so much worse, but God. …God intervened. He stepped in and sent so many in her path to lighten her way and help her to see the wiles and schemes of the devil.

After she spoke at the sisters' prayer breakfast, a woman prophesied to Charisma. She pulled her aside and said, "Baby, there is always a crushing before the anointing."

"Ma'am?" Charisma questioned, not sure what she meant by her comment.

The kind lady smiled and took Charisma's hand in hers as they sat together on the pew. The talking and excitement of all the other ladies buzzed around them.

She repeated herself again, "There is always a crushing before the anointing. What I mean by that is there is obviously something huge about to come about into your life, sweet girl. You have not gone through all this for no reason at all.

If you read in Exodus, anointing oil was made with specific spices and herbs. But the anointing oil wasn't made just by pouring the spices and herbs into some oils and letting that be it. No. Not even letting it sit for days or months was going to cause that anointing oil to be what it is meant to be. The herbs and spices that helped make the anointing oil needed to be crushed first. It needed to be completely crushed down to grains which opened up the beautiful scent that was trapped inside it. Then those herbs could be poured into the oil and sit, which helped the oil become the true anointing oil it was intended to be. It could never become its greatest form unless the herbs were crushed first. The beautiful scent could have never emerged unless they were first crushed.

Do you understand what I'm saying, honey?"

Charisma nodded her head in awe at how well she really understood what this lady was saying. It was as if God Himself came down from heaven and stood in this lady's place and spoke directly to her. It was as if she was speaking into her soul. She could hear, feel, and envision things that she never saw before.

This moment was so surreal for Charisma. In a flash, Charisma saw her future as this lady spoke. She saw herself speaking to women in a huge auditorium. She also saw herself sitting at a table signing books. She couldn't understand what it was for or about, but she knew it was God showing her herself, and she trusted Him.

"You are and have been experiencing a crushing. It's unlike anything you have ever experienced before. The bigger the crushing, baby, sometimes the bigger the anointing. So, what I'm saying is - get ready. Prepare yourself. There's no time to sit around and twiddle your thumbs.

You've got work to do because you will and are already being used by God. Look at what you've done here today. You think these young girls will ever forget this message you brought here? You are allowing yourself to be used in a mighty way.

You could be hiding away, pregnant in shame. But no, you are uncovering everything the enemy wants to hide, and you are exposing it all for the glory of our Lord. You are fighting the good fight, and I'm here for it, baby."

She held Charisma's little hand in hers then kissed the back of it. She put her hand back down on her lap and patted it, silently smiling at Charisma for a moment.

It was as if in that moment, they both were allowed to see something that no one else in the room could see. It was like they had a complete understanding that God was moving, and things were beginning to shift in the atmosphere.

At home that night, Charisma was sitting on her windowsill remembering that conversation with sister Betty. She was watching the rain drops as they fell and hit her glass window one by one. Some bigger than others. She pulled out her pad and began to write.

The rain drops all come from the same place. The Sky...

They all have the same opportunities, to become something bigger than themselves. Not all raindrops end up performing the same tasks. Some become part of lakes and others, rivers. Some raindrops become a part of something really great, like the ocean. Some, though from the same place, fall and hit only the ground, or my glass window. Slowly sliding down into nothingness.

It's not that they couldn't be great oceans or rivers like the other raindrops became, it just so happened that's where that specific one landed. It was the cards that were dealt to them. So, it made the best of what it had and when that specific raindrop hit the pavement instead of an ocean or a river, it made the biggest splash and loudest noise it could. Showing that it was there.

When the one hit my glass window as I watched it slide down to my windowsill, it might not have slid down into a puddle, but it made the most beautiful patterns as it did its thing and slid down to its destiny.

The point is - some raindrops become part of something that may seem big or great to some. But don't underestimate the greatness in the splash or patterns left behind in others.

Don't focus on where you land…just MAKE…YOUR LANDING… GREAT!

Charisma put down her pen and pad and leaned her head against the wall of her room. She continued to watch the beauty in the drops that instead of being part of something as great as becoming bigger than themselves like an ocean, these drops were doing something great for her. They were calming her. Their sounds were lulling her to sleep. They were fulfilling their destiny and becoming part of something bigger and great, but so very different from what other raindrops may expect or want to be for themselves.

Suddenly, Charisma jumped! She grabbed for her dress trying to understand exactly what just moved between her thighs. She felt something move along the side of her leg and she jumped to stand up. Charisma had never had a baby before, so everything was new to her. She didn't understand that the feeling down the inside of her leg was her water breaking until she stood up completely and more began to trickle down.

"Oh, my goodness!" Charisma shouted in a panic. "Mom! Dad!"

Charisma's parents came rushing into her bedroom. They found her standing in shock with her legs open in a football stance and a crazed daze.

"It's okay, Charisma. Your water just broke. Let's get you to the hospital. You're going to be okay. Just breathe."

As Charisma breathed, panic still overwhelmed her as contractions hit quickly. She was close to having a fit until she heard her mother near her quoting scripture and praying over her.

Immediately, Charisma felt peace. The kind the bible talks about that says, "peace that passeth all understanding." It made no sense as to why she was all of a sudden calm. But the moment she heard her mom praying, it was all well in her soul.

She calmly put on her shoes and walked downstairs to the car with her dad's help. They quietly made their way to the hospital.

CHAPTER THIRTY - THREE
EXODUS

Charisma was back in her hospital room still taking in all the moments that transpired that landed her here.

"I'm a mother," she whispered to herself.

She slowly got out of the bed, walked over to her baby, and looked him over from head to toe. She was so amazed by God and His goodness. It made her emotional just to stand over her new baby boy and see how much love she had for him, even though he was conceived through tragedy.

She was able to look at him and see pure love and not be reminded of anything else. *"That could be nothing else but God,"* Charisma thought as she smiled to herself.

She unswaddled him so she could get a better look at him. She wanted to inspect her little bundle of joy. When she took his left leg out from the little swaddle, she noticed a mark on his leg. It was like a birthmark in the shape of an X. It was so pronounced that she couldn't take her eyes off the mark for a while.

Then it hit her. Charisma finally knew her baby's name...

It was Exodus!

CHAPTER THIRTY- FOUR
MY FREEDOM STORY

While studying at the library one day, a woman leaned over her carriage and smiled at the baby. She whispered, "What a good baby, so quiet."

"Yes, thank you. He's very good. I got so very blessed with him."

"Oh, it's a boy? What's his name?" The woman inquired.

"Exodus."

The woman stopped and stared at her. The once kind gesture and admiring smile she had turned into a slight frown. "His name is Exodus? Like Exodus from the Bible?"

"Yes ma'am," Charisma responded with such pride. She was accustomed to this kind of reaction and for the most part, expected it by now. Usually some of the younger generation thought it was cool, but most of the older ones questioned her decisions.

Funnily, her parents never did. They never looked at her with confusion when she announced the name to them. Actually, they seemed proud. When she broke it all down to them, they beamed with pride in their daughter and her choice. But it wasn't her choice. It was the name God had given her for her son, and she knew in this new season of her life - obedience was key.

No matter what she was feeling or how uncomfortable something might be for her - if God sent her, she went. Told her to do, she did. Any and everything that was directed by God for her, Charisma was obedient.

It was her gratefulness to God and His grace for her that drove her on a daily basis. It's what drove her now in these long days at the library and staying up long nights at home writing papers for her theology classes.

Charisma had received her call into ministry. She heard it loud and clear and was going all in full speed ahead, being a young mom and all. It didn't matter. She knew He was going to make a way and get her through. She had a testimony to tell; she had people to teach. She had a word for the lost and time was of the essence. She was on a mission. A mission to serve God.

"His name is EXODUS; we call him X for short."

"You mean like Malcolm X?"

"NO. I mean like X in Exodus," as she looks down and points to her baby. "He is MY story of freedom...Would you like me to tell you about it?"

CHAPTER THIRTY- FIVE
LIFE

"Today, I would like to tell you a little story about LIFE," Charisma began as she walked out onto one of the biggest platforms she had ever spoken on before. She looked around and realized how magnificent our God truly is.

"Pray with me before we get started, would you? Lord, You showed me this moment, Father. Years ago, when sister Betty took my hand and spoke life into and over me. You showed me this exact moment and I never doubted that it was a vision from You. Now to stand here in this place, before these individuals, and be living it is so surreal but so detailed and orchestrated by You.

I know there is something very special that You would have for me to bring to these individuals today. I sense that someone, or maybe someone(s), are in real need of the word that is being brought today. Father, I ask that, as Your word is the living word, that You will come alive within each and every individual under my voice.

Anoint the words You've given me, Lord. I pray that this word will move upon us. Allow it to work in each person's heart and life in a way that fits them specifically. Make it clear, Lord, like only You can. I pray, Father, for obedience within me. To say only what You have called me to say and to leave out all that You choose to be left out. I do this for You, Father. So, I decrease that You will increase. Less of me and so so much more of You, God. I pray this and all things in Christ Jesus name, and we all say, Amen.

One day there were three individuals who worked together in a factory. Their job was to stand and hold up four letters all day. The letters they worked to hold up were L, I, F, and E.

Each person held up their LIFE day in and day out. When their shift was over, they would sit their LIFE down in the booth and go home. Only to come back and do it all again the next day.

One day, Person 1 got off early and sat down her LIFE in the booth, locked up, and headed out. As she passed Person 2, she stopped to wave and chat for a bit while he sat his LIFE down and locked up too. She kept walking only to notice that Person 3 was still holding up her LIFE and looked sad. She told herself not to worry about it and went home.

The next day, they all got back to work, opened up their assigned booths, picked up their own LIFE and held it up. 1 and 2 held up their LIFE with no problem as they usually did but there was 3 again struggling.

Person 1 just couldn't understand it, but she ignored it. She went along with holding up her LIFE and smiled so brightly. Her life was so shiny it brought her so much joy to hold up her LIFE. She couldn't help but smile.

When that shift was over, 1 put her LIFE down carefully and lovingly and began to lock up. She waved at 2 as she walked past because 2 was packing up to leave as well. But then she noticed 3 again. Something about 3 always made her feel so sorry for her. 3 was still standing, struggling to hold up her LIFE. She didn't look like she was getting off anytime soon.

She prayed and asked, "God, why does 3 suffer so much? We all hold up our LIFE just like the others, we have the same amount of letters. I don't understand why her LIFE seems so much more of a struggle than ours. Why does her LIFE not look as shiny as mine or 2's?

God answered, "It's just the LIFE she was given. Each of you are given your own LIFE, and you have to carry it no matter what it looks like. It's just the way it is."

"But God, that just seems so unfair. I just don't understand. Why do I have a shiny LIFE, and she has such a gloomy looking LIFE? It just doesn't make sense to me."

"LIFE won't always make sense to your natural way of thinking, my child. Think spiritually and maybe it will become more clear to you."

So that night, 1 tossed and turned all night thinking about what God said. She prayed, she read scripture, and finally was able to fall asleep and get some rest. On her way in that morning, she cheerfully waved at 3 who had started early holding up her LIFE, but 3 didn't respond. She thought, "well, geesh, that's so rude. No wonder LIFE is hard for her. She's so mean.

1's feelings were so hurt she didn't know what to think. She tried to shake it off and pick up her shiny LIFE again and get her own day started.

After another long day of doing LIFE again, they were done. So, 1 packed up, sat her LIFE down carefully as she always did, locked up her booth, and headed out. She waved as she walked past 2 beginning to sit down his LIFE. When she walked past 3, she could smell a harsh smell coming from 3's booth and she thought, "wow God, her LIFE really stinks." She held her nose and tried to walk by quickly so as not to breathe in the pungent smell anymore. But then she stopped and really looked at 3.

She realized 3 was always facing the opposite direction from 1 and 2 so she could never see her face. She took the time to walk around to the other side. For the first time, she noticed the pain in 3's face. She could see how heavy her LIFE was. It truly looked like at any moment her LIFE was going to crush her. 1 felt so sorry for her that she decided to step into the messy, stinky, yucky booth with 3.

As 1 stepped into 3's booth, 3 looked over at her in shock, but also with embarrassment. 1 realized that 3 was ashamed of her LIFE and would never ask for help because of that shame. 1 looked 3 in the eyes and smiled at her as she grabbed her L and held the L up with her. 3 felt a small relief in her legs. For the first time, 3 was able to stand a bit straighter.

2 had been watching the whole thing and took example from 1 and climbed into the booth too. He stood on the other side of 3, looked at her and took her E from her.

She looked at him with tears in her eyes. For the first time, in what seemed like forever, 3 was able to stand completely straight up. 1 noticed that the smell in the booth seemed to get a little better. It didn't seem as dark and gloomy in there as it was before.

They both noticed 3 looked even taller than before. They never realized how tall 3 was before because she was always so bent over by the way LIFE had been weighing her down. She stood so tall that her 2 letters that she was left holding, the I and the F, were so far above the E and the L that it spelt out IF. Then, for the first time, 3 began to speak.

"What IF LIFE isn't so bad? What IF LIFE can be good? What IF LIFE could shine bright for me like it does for others? What IF?"

In that very moment, 3 began to turn. 1 and 2 followed her lead and turned with her until she was finally, for the first time, facing the correct direction. She took her L from 1 and her E from 2 and thanked them.

"Thank you both for your help. No one has ever done for me what you two have done. You have blessed me in such a way. You took time away from your own LIFE to step into my mess and help me carry my LIFE. Then, you didn't stop there. You helped me to turn my LIFE around. Thank you so very much, I will never forget either of you.

1 finally got the lesson. She realized that we can't continue to do LIFE alone. There is no satisfaction there just looking at your shiny LIFE all day. Sometimes we need to step into the mess with a friend. Just long enough to help them turn their LIFE around.

CHAPTER THIRTY - SIX
HER STORY…HISTORY…HIS STORY

Charisma meets a young, pregnant girl at the conference and speaks LIFE into her. The cycle continues.

LIFE is not by coincidence. We are all spiritually connected.

"I love you, mommy!" "X" yells from the front row, bouncing and waving happily on Ivan's lap.

"I love you more, X!"

That's something he had always done since he could speak, and she never stopped him. No matter where she was, if X told his mom he loved her, and she could hear him, she responded back with love. He was always and forever going to know that this mother had and will continue to have his back.

This was her Exodus! A Young Girls Journey to Freedom!

Simone K. Baker

EXODUS

Dear Reader,

Thank you for picking up this book. Whether you found this book on your own or if my book found you, it's not by coincidence.

Sister, we have a connection to one another in some way or another. Although this book and the life of this sweet girl Charisma is a fictional story, there are some true moments throughout. True in that you may see yourself in some of the experiences Charisma has been through. Or you may have met some of the characters she has come across. I know I have. There's a few of Charisma's experiences that I personally can say I see myself in and maybe you do too.

Life isn't easy but we live life for a purpose. Our purpose is to grow the kingdom of God.

What I want to impress upon you in this moment is…. we are a sisterhood. Whether I know you personally or not, you are my sister, and I love you. Know that your life experiences are connected to someone else. It's not all about you. There's a purpose behind your pain.

You may not know it now but pray and ask God for clarity about why you had to take this route. Or why you're in the process of living this life right now.

You will find that it's connected to someone else. Another sister who needs you. She needs to learn from your mistakes or gain faith from your testimony. None of your life is by mistake or coincidence. It's all for a purpose. HIS purpose... and that's to grow HIS kingdom.

Pay attention to the sisters around you. Lend a helping hand when needed or a silent prayer. Make sure your prayers are loaded in great faith because that's how He answers, when your great faith is connected.

Believe, ladies. Believe that things will always turn for HIS good which is also your good. In the end, it will bring our Father His glory.

Love you,

Your big sister in Christ
Simone

MEET THE AUTHOR

Simone was born in Hartford Connecticut. At 2 years old her grandmother took custody of her and raised her through her adolescent years. She is now her grandmother's caregiver and is blessed to be able to care for her as she cared for Simone.

In 2006, Simon married Thurman Baker, and they have five amazing children.

In 2021, Simone graduated with her Bachelor's in Ministry from Palm Beach Atlantic University where she was ordained on December 10, 2021. Shortly after, Simone joined the staff of The Father's House as one of the Associate Pastors.

Simone owns a salon in Leesburg and works with young adults in the church and the community. She has a passion for leading people to Christ and helping them discover their purpose!

BOOK DISCUSSION QUESTIONS

1. What part of Charisma's story did you relate to most?

2. Do you think Charisma was too judgmental of Dafney?

3. Have you ever felt trapped in a situation?

4. Have you ever pushed someone away out of pride or feeling unworthy?

5. Do you or have you had any Franky's in your life? Egotistical, manipulative, etc.

6. Have you ever experienced something that caused you to feel as though you had nothing left to offer or that you were no longer useful or good?

7. What do you think the journal entry "Rain" was truly about?

8. What is your overall takeaway from Charisma's story and how has it helped you?

Made in the USA
Middletown, DE
03 September 2024

60254681R00129